Frank glim n
his hands and pt
clear of him. vn
man, but the ly
defensive—maybe waiting for reinforcements?
Frank wondered.

"I can't quite get that . . . six bind," panted
Rutledge. "How do you . . . take the blade to
start it?"

"Watch," called Frank. He hopped forward,
took his opponent's sword from below, and
then whirled his point in around the other man's
bell guard; he lunged, and the point punctured
the eye and the brain of the unfortunate Transport.

"Thus," said Frank, holding the position for
Rutledge's benefit. "Begin it like a standard
counter six. And finish with a moderate lunge."

"I see," said Rutledge. Frank straightened
up to watch his pupil. After a moment the thief-
lord leaped forward, caught the man's blade,
and, lunging, spun his point into the man's eye.
The Transport dropped like a puppet with its
strings cut.

"Well done, my lord!" Frank nodded. "You
see the advantage of practice."

used the Transam, who was ...
... knees on the pavement, and kep...
... Frank tried two feints on his own ...
... the policeman was being carted ...

FORSAKE THE SKY

TIM POWERS

A TOM DOHERTY ASSOCIATES BOOK

FORSAKE THE SKY

Copyright © 1976, 1986 by Tim Powers

This edition has been revised from THE SKIES DISCROWNED, published by Laser Books, 1976.

First printing: April 1986

A TOR Book

Published by Tom Doherty Associates
49 West 24 Street
New York, N.Y. 10010

Cover art by Boris Vallejo

ISBN: 0-812-54973-2
CAN. ED.: 0-812-54974-0

Printed in the United States

0 9 8 7 6 5 4 3 2 1

To Roy A. Squires

BOOK ONE: The Painter

Chapter 1

Dominion, it was called—a network that eventually encompassed a hundred stars in a field five thousand light-years across—and it was the most ambitious social experiment humans had ever embarked upon. It was a nation of more than a hundred planets, united by the Transport spaceships, the freighters that made possible the complex economic equations of supply and demand that kept the unthinkably vast Dominion empire running smoothly. Food from the fertile plains and seas of planets like Earth was shipped out to the worlds that produced ore, or vacuum-and-low-gravity industry, or simply provided office space; and the machinery and nutrients and pesticides from the manufactory worlds kept the farm worlds functioning at peak efficiency. Planetary independence was a necessity of the past—now no planet's government need struggle to be self-sufficient; each world simply produced the things it was best

3

*suited to, and relied on the Transport ships to pro-
vide such necessities as were lacking.*

*For centuries Dominion was a healthy organism,
nourished by its varied and widespread resources,
which the bloodstream of the Transport ships distrib-
uted to all its parts.*

FRANK Rovzar sat slouched against the back of the
horse-drawn cart, hemmed in by a dozen hot, un-
happy kitchen servants. They were all moaning and
asking each other questions that none of them knew
the answers to: Where are we going? What happened? Who are these people? Frank was the only
silent one in the cart; he sat where he'd been thrown,
staring intensely at nothing. From time to time he
flexed his tightly bound wrists.

The cart rattled along southward on the Cromlech
Road, making good time, for the Cromlech was one
of the few highways on the planet that received
regular maintenance. Within two hours of leaving the
devastated palace they had arrived at the Barclay Transport Depot southwest of Munson, by the banks of the
Malachi River. The cart, along with fifteen others
like it, was taken through a gate in the chain-link
fence that enclosed the depot, and across the wide,
scorched concrete plain, and finally was brought to a
halt in front of a bleak gray four-storey edifice.

Small-cargo scales had been dragged up from somewhere and now stood in a row by the doors. The
bedraggled occupants of the carts were pulled and
prodded out onto the pavement, weighed, lined up
according to sex and mass, and then divided into
groups and escorted into the building.

AFTER *many centuries and dozens of local Golden
Ages, Dominion began to weaken. It had expanded*

too rapidly, and the expected breakthroughs in faster-than-light communication and portable nuclear-fusion reactors simply never happened. Fossil fuels and Uranium-235 were inadequate in quantity and distribution. Transportation became increasingly expensive, and many things were no longer worth shipping. The smooth pulse of the import/export network had taken on a lurching, strained pace.

"NAME." The officer's voice had no intonation.

"Francisco de Goya Rovzar."

"Age."

"Twenty."

"Occupation."

"Uh . . . apprentice painter."

"Okay, Rovzar, step over there with the others."

Frank walked away from the desk and joined a crowd of other prisoners. The room they were in seemed calculated to induce depression. The floor was of damp cement, with drains set in at regular intervals; the paint was blistering off the pale green walls; the ceiling was corrugated aluminum, and naked light bulbs swung on the ends of long cords in the perpetual chilly draft.

The perfunctory interrogation continued until all the prisoners taken that morning had been questioned and stood in a milling, spiritless crowd. The officer who had been asking the questions now stood up and, flanked by two others who carried machine guns, faced the prisoners. He was short, with close-cropped sandy hair and a bristly moustache; his uniform was faultlessly neat.

"Give me your attention for a moment," he said, unnecessarily. "You are here as prisoners of the Transport Authority, and of Costa, who two hours ago was confirmed as the new Duke of this planet.

Ordinarily each of you would be allowed a court hearing in which to contest the charge of treason laid against you, but the entire planet of Octavio has, as of this morning, been declared to be under martial law." He was reciting all this as dispassionately as a tired waiter announcing that the daily special is all gone. "When this condition is lifted you will be free to appeal your sentence. The sentence, like the crime, is the same for each of you: you are to be lifted tomorrow on a Transport freighter and ferried to the Orestes system to atone for your offenses in the uranium industry. Are there any questions?"

There were none. A few people laughed incredulously, for it was actually illegal for uranium miners to reenter normal society. Frank, his mind only now beginning to recover from the shock of his father's murder, heard the sentence, but its irony, whether intentional or just negligent, was wasted on him. He filed the news away without thinking about it.

THE situation did not improve. Transportation became more and more sporadic and unreliable. Industrial planets were often left for weeks without food shipments, and agricultural planets were unable to replace broken machinery or obtain fuel for what worked. The Transport Company was losing its grip on the wide-flung empire; the outer sections were dying. Transport rates climbed, and the poorer planets, unable to maintain contact with the Dominion, were forced to drop out and try to survive alone. In time even the richest planets began working to be self-sufficient, in case the Transport Company should one day collapse entirely.

LATE that night Frank sat awake in the darkness of one of the depot detention pens. His cot and thin mattress were not particularly uncomfortable, but his thoughts were too vivid and alarming for him to sleep. The six other men in the pen with him apparently didn't care to think, and slept deeply.

My father is dead, Frank told himself; but he couldn't really believe it yet, not emotionally. Impressions of his father alive were too strong—he could still see the old man laughing over a mug of beer in a tavern, or sketching strangers' faces in a pocket notebook, or shaking Frank awake in the predawn dimness so that they could gulp some coffee while they bundled up canvas and brushes and paints and thinners before getting on the horses and galloping off somewhere to catch a subject in the perfect light. Frank thought of how his life would be without old Rovzar to take care of, and he shied away from the lonely vision.

His destination was the Orestes mines. That was bad—about as bad as it could be. The mines riddled all four planets of the relatively young Orestes system, and working conditions ranged from desiccating desert heat to cold that could kill an exposed man in seconds. But the sovereign danger—and eventual certainty—was radiation poisoning. Panic grew in him as it became clear that he was about to be devastatingly punished by men who had never seen him before and were totally indifferent to him.

Only this morning—or was it now past midnight? Probably; only yesterday morning, then—he'd been playing with practice weapons at the Strand Fencing Academy. Now in this disinfectant-smelling darkness he wondered how he could have failed to see the shadow of the world's true nature in the formalities of the stylized combat—the points and edges were imaginary, but the foils were models of a killing-tool

. . . a killing-tool every bit as real and routinely used as the pot in which a cook boils lobsters.

His father's appointment with Duke Topo—Costa's father—hadn't been until noon, and the portrait his father was doing was well under way and needed no particular preparation from the apprentice, so Frank had strapped his foil and mask to the back of his saddle and ridden to Strand's.

The place was just one room, but it was huge, a hundred feet by a hundred feet, with a ceiling so far above the floor that in decades no one had brushed the ropy cobwebs away from the very highest frames and trophies. A class was in session when Frank arrived, so he sat down on a bench between two of the tall windows and watched the sons of the aristocracy hop and plunge and flail about. He hoped it was a beginners' class. The classes were getting bigger; a generation or two ago the young men were all taking shooting lessons.

When old Strand finally declared the lesson ended and told the students to pair off and bout with one another, and warned them which moves they weren't to attempt yet, he walked over to Frank's bench.

"Hello, Frankie. Looking for a bout?"

"Yes sir. Is Tom around?"

"No, I sent the boy off on some errands. I'll go around with you, though, if you like."

"Well . . . okay."

It was always intimidating to fence with Tom's father, for the old man would frequently halt a bout to point out, loudly, his opponent's errors, and if the opponent managed to score even one touch against old Strand's five it was a rare feat; but it was true too that one's next opponent, no matter who it was, seemed much less daunting.

Frank was left-handed, and once they'd found a

vacant strip, put on their masks and jackets, saluted and come on guard, he kept his blade well-extended in an exaggeratedly outside-twisted *sixte* position, for this pretty much forced the right-hander to attack into his inside line, and it was such a long way to reach that Frank could generally let an incoming blade come close enough to be totally committed before he parried, and thus he wasted a lot less effort—and exposure—trying to parry thrusts that turned out to be mere feints.

But it did little good against Tom's father, who could, almost supernaturally, wait until the last split instant before deciding whether his attack *was* genuine, or just a feint to open Frank's defenses for an attack somewhere else. Frank took four touches in two minutes, and his only consolation was that the old man once shouted "Not bad!" when a compound riposte of Frank's nearly hit him.

After the fourth touch Strand stepped back. "Have you been practicing the Self-Inflicted Foot Thrust?" he asked. His voice, it seemed to Frank, was as relaxed as if he'd just now looked up from reading a book.

"Well," Frank panted, "yeah—some."

"Put me into it."

"Okay." Frank took a deep breath and then hopped backward, his sword raised; Strand beat it aside and advanced with a thrust; Frank caught the older man's blade in a bind from below, whipped it upward with his own blade, and then flung it downward; but not only did Strand's point fail to strike Strand's own foot, as it would have if Frank had done the move correctly, but Strand's blade had lashed back up, knocked Frank's aside, and then darted in to flex firmly against Frank's chest.

"Not yet, lad." Strand laughed, flipping his mask

back and stepping forward to shake hands. "But keep practicing it."

"Yes sir."

As Frank turned away he saw that Strand's son Tom had returned sometime during the bout and was now grinning and shaking his head at him. "At least," he called cheerfully to Frank, "you almost hit your *own* foot that time."

"You want to fence," Frank asked with a defiant smile, "or just stand there and criticize your betters?"

"Might as well play *chess* as fence with those *foils*," said Tom, nevertheless crossing to the weapons rack. "That kind of fencing's got no bearing on real sword-fighting." He spoke almost automatically, for this was just one more thrust in a long-standing argument between Tom and Frank. Tom was always emphasizing the combat aspects of the sport, and talking about edges and points and blood-channels. He insisted that, to have any real value, fencing should approximate as closely as possible the conditions of real sword-fighting: the weapons should be heavier, the boundary lines on the floor dispensed with, "off-target" touches acknowledged with some physical handicap like an imposed limp and a bleed-to-death time limit. Frank usually countered by pretending to agree enthusiastically and then going on to suggest that touched fencers be required to groan, too, and fall dramatically, and maybe splash some artificial blood on the touched spot.

Generally Frank refused to do any saber fencing with Tom, for the fencing master's son tended to lean into the blows too much—even though Frank nearly always won, his back and arms would be welted afterward from hits that, though mis-timed or delivered after valid hits of Frank's, nevertheless stung; but today, with Tom still grinning reminiscently about

Frank's failure at the Self-Inflicted Foot Thrust, he wanted to beat him at something Tom considered worthwhile.

"Okay," he said carelessly, "dig out a couple of sabers, then."

Tom laughed in surprise. "All *right*! You want to lose at something that *counts*, eh?" He swerved toward the saber-and-épée cabinet, digging in his pocket for his keys.

"Something . . . not too abstract," said Frank. "Hell, you'd probably be good at chess, too, if you could always use pieces that were made to look like little people."

Tom Strand had found the right key, and he unlocked the cabinet and swung its door open. "Well," he began, his smile a little forced now, "at least—at least I—"

"And if they bleated when you knocked them over," Frank went on, "like those little perforated cans they give to kids, where each one makes the noise of the animal whose picture's on the outside. A bishop could, like, make praying noises when you tipped him over, and the queen could yell rape or something—"

Tom selected a saber and then looked at Frank. He was squinting in what Frank had come to recognize as his man-of-the-world style. "Take a flight a few thousand feet over Munson," he advised. "The streets look as ordered and geometrical as a checkerboard. But then come down and look closer." He whirled his saber through the air fast enough to make it whistle. "The universe is one big jungle, and you've got to—"

"I know," said Frank wearily as he took a left-handed blade for himself, "become a jungle creature to survive. I bet you use camouflage-pattern condoms.''

Tom laughed delightedly, and then winked at Frank. ''You think it's *my* idea? They *demand* 'em.''

''Snake women you hang out with,'' said Frank. ''They'd like you even better with a set of rattles.''

The conversation deteriorated even further then as their friendship and humor smoothed over the momentary edginess, and soon they were masked and slashing enthusiastically at each other as they stamped back and forth along one of the fencing strips. Frank beat Tom in the first bout, and in the second one they lost track of the score and just fenced until Frank had to leave to meet his father and ride to the palace.

Tom Strand hadn't, this time, wielded the saber as if he were trying to beat dust out of a carpet, and as Frank rode home he reflected that even Tom was beginning to realize that it could be a civilized sport.

SOMEONE in a nearby cell whimpered now in the darkness, and Frank wondered whether the man's nightmare could possibly be worse than what he'd presently be waking up to. Frank remembered young Costa's grunt of effort as he drove the blade of his dress sword into his own father's belly; a civilized sport, he thought.

Chapter 2

Only in death had Topo, the old Duke, taken on any dignity in Frank's eyes; before he was murdered by his son he had always seemed to be nothing more than a caricature of a planetary duke—either draping his ludicrously fat body in multicolored jewelled robes in order to ride a gaudy float in a parade or to publicly sign some obscure proclamation, or disappearing into the Ducal Palace to indulge himself in his dining room and harem. Rumor had it that even in the harem the old Duke would not permit himself to be seen without a suitable tunic and turban; the more utilitarian of his visits there were said to be conducted in absolute darkness to preserve the dignity of his station.

When Frank's father had begun doing the old Duke's portrait two weeks ago, the old painter had jokingly suggested that the Duke pose nude. Frank, who'd been setting up the easel, actually thought for a moment that Topo was going to have his father flung

out of the palace. The Duke had managed to swallow
his rage, though, and then force a laugh and decline
the offer, but it was lucky that Frank's father had
been in the early, blocking-in-with-pencil stage of the
portrait, for Topo's face didn't lose its redness during
that entire session.

Only at one other session had Frank's father apparently deviated from strictly respectful professional-
ism; Frank wasn't sure, for he didn't understand the
bit of dialogue he'd overheard when he returned,
more quickly than usual, from a turpentine-fetching
errand. On their way home that evening Frank had
asked his father about it, but the old painter had just
laughed and said he couldn't discuss it, that it was a
state secret. Frank had puzzled over it later. "Sure
you don't want me to make it either all-bird or
all-girl?" his father had muttered quietly to the Duke,
before either of them had noticed that Frank had
returned. "I still could, you know." The Duke had
replied with some remark about a stretched canvas,
and then saw Frank and hastily changed the subject.

The session yesterday, which had ended with the
murders of Topo and old Rovzar, had begun ordinarily. The guards at the barbican gate had recognized
the old painter and his son, and waved the pair on
inside with sociably slack slingshots. The wait in
front of the palace doors was perhaps a little longer
than usual, but they were in the cool shadow of the
wall, and the page who took their horse brought them
a bucket of chilly beer and two wooden mugs when
he returned, and they used the extra time to comb
their sweaty hair and stamp some of the road dust off
their boots.

At last the doors were unbolted from the inside and
swung open by an expressionless guard—Frank thought
now that it had not been the usual doorguard—who

beckoned them inside and escorted them up the stairs and along the familiar hall to the throne room. The man pulled the doors open for them and stepped back, and Frank, getting a fresh grip on the satchel of painting supplies, followed his father inside.

"Ah, there you are, Rovzar!" boomed Duke Topo from the tall chair of mosaic-inlaid ebony in the center of the room. As usual for these sessions, his bulky person was enclosed in a baggy pair of blue silk trousers and a green velvet coat. Ringlets of hair, so shiny as to seem varnished, covered his head and clustered about his shoulders.

"Your Grace," acknowledged the older Rovzar. Father and son both bowed. The room was lit by tall, open windows in the eastern wall; bookcases hid the other three walls, and a desk and chair were set in one corner. In the middle of the room, facing the throne in which the Duke sat, was a wooden stand supporting a canvas five feet tall and three feet wide. The canvas, which was framed temporarily in plain wood, was the nearly finished portrait of the Duke, done in oils. It presented him dressed and seated as he now was, but it conveyed a dignity and strength, even a touch of sadness, that were lacking in the model.

"You think you'll finish it this session?" the Duke asked.

"It's not unlikely," answered Frank's father. "But I can't say for sure, of course."

"Of course," nodded the Duke.

Old Rovzar put his hand on his son's shoulder. "Okay, now, Frank," he said, "you set up the palette and turp and oil while I say hello to the picture." He crossed to the painting and stood in front of it, staring intently. Frank unbuckled the satchel, set up a small folding table and laid out on it a dozen

crumpled paint tubes, then poured linseed oil and
turpentine into two metal cups. He unwound a rubber
band from a bundle of brushes and set them in another cup. A young page, standing beside the sitting
Duke, looked on with great interest.

The doors opened and a slim, pale young man
entered. He wore powder blue tights and a matching
tunic with ruffles at the throat. A fancy-hilted sword
hung at his belt.

"Costa, my boy!" greeted the Duke. "Finished
with your piano lesson so soon?"

"I despise pianos," the prince informed him. "Is
he still working on that picture?" He walked over
and peered closely at the canvas. "Hmmm," he
grunted, before turning and walking to the window.
His attitude implied that this painting wasn't bad, in
a provincial way, but that he'd frequently seen better.
Frank remembered the prince's tantrums after he had
been told that he was not to be included in the
painting—for a week Costa had sulked, and then in
the days since tried to make it clear that he regarded
Rovzar as an inferior painter.

Frank's father was sketching lightly in a background area of the canvas, oblivious to the world.
*What is it that's different about young Prince Costa
this morning?* Frank had wondered. *He's quiet, for
one thing; usually he makes himself tiresome with
frequent questions and distractions.* Frank suppressed
a smile as he remembered one day when Costa had
brought a drawing pad and pastels and made an
attempt to portray the Duke himself, with much squinting and many theatrical gestures. But now he simply
stood at the window, staring down into the courtyard.

Frank's attention was caught by his father's block-
ing in of the background. With a few passes of a
pencil the artist's hand had converted a patch of

blank canvas into several bookshelves in perfect perspective. He set about defining the shadows with quick cross-hatching.

Suddenly it occurred to Frank what was different about Prince Costa. This was the first time Frank had seen him wearing a sword.

"Where's my number eight camel hair?" asked old Rovzar, pawing through the brushes. "Right here, Dad," replied Frank, pointing out the one in question. "Oh, yes." The painter took the brush, dipped it into the linseed oil, and began mixing a dab of paint.

A loud bang echoed up from the courtyard.

"What was that?" asked the Duke.

Several more bangs rattled the glass in the windows, then there was a series of them like a string of firecrackers going off.

"By God," said Frank, "I think it's *gunfire*." He spoke incredulously, guns and powder being so prohibitively rare and expensive these days. Panicky yells sounded, punctuated by more shots.

"We're beset!" gasped the Duke. Prince Costa ran out of the room, and the Duke took his place at the window. "Troops!" he shouted. "A hundred Transport soldiers are within the bailey!"

Old Rovzar looked up. "What?" he asked. "I trust my painting won't be interrupted?"

"Interrupted?" The Duke waved his fists. "The Transports will probably use your canvas to polish their boots!" An explosion shook the palace, and the Duke scrambled back from the window. The pandemonium of shouts, shots and screams was a mounting roar.

The Duke ran bobbing and puffing across the carpeted floor to the desk. He yanked out drawers and began throwing bundles of letters and documents in a pile on the floor. "How did they get *in*?" he kept whining. "How in the devil's name did they get *in*?"

Frank glanced at his father. "Do we run for it?" he asked tensely. The young page stared at them with wide eyes.

Frank's father scratched his chin. "No, I guess not. We're better off here than down in that madhouse of a courtyard. Just don't panic. Damn, I hope nobody sticks a bayonet through this," he said, staring at the painting.

The hollow booms of two more explosions jarred Frank's teeth. "This attack must be costing a fortune," he said, awed.

The Duke had struck a match and set it to his pile of papers; most of them were yellowed with age, and they were consumed quickly, scorching the rug under them. When they had burned to fragile black curls he stamped them into powder. "What else, what else?" the distraught Duke moaned, wringing his hands.

Suddenly from beyond the throne room doors Frank heard a hoarse, triumphant yell, and then heavy-booted footsteps running up the hall toward the room they were in. The page ran to the doors and threw a more-or-less decorative-looking bolt into the locked position.

The Duke had heard it too and sprang to one of the bookcases. His pudgy hands snatched one of the books from the shelf, and then he stood holding it, staring wildly around the room. The attackers were pounding on the doors now. The Duke's eyes lit on the painting and he ran to it with a glad cry. He stuffed the book—which, Frank noticed, was a leather-bound copy of *Winnie the Pooh*—behind the picture's frame, so that it lay hidden between the canvas and the thick cross-bracing. This done, he ran back to his throne and sat down, exhausted. Frank and the old painter stared at him, even in this crisis puzzled by the Duke's action.

Six bullets splintered downward through the doors, one snapping the bolt and two more tearing through the page's chest, the impact throwing him to the floor. Frank's numbed mind had time to be amazed at the quickness of it.

The doors were kicked open and a dozen men strode into the room. Eleven of them were soldiers who wore the gray Transport uniform and carried rifles, but it was the twelfth, the apparent leader, who held the attention of Rovzar, his son and the Duke.

"Costa!" exclaimed the astounded Duke. "Not you . . . ?"

Costa drew his sword with a sharp rasp of steel. "On guard, your Grace," he whispered tightly, holding the blade forward and crouching a bit. Terrible form, thought Frank.

It was adequate against the Duke, though, whose only defensive action was to cover his face with his hands. Prince Costa hesitated, his face palely blotchy and his sword trembling, then cursed and drove the blade into Duke Topo's chest. He wrenched it out, and the Duke sighed and bowed forward, leaning farther and farther, until he overbalanced and tumbled messily to the floor.

One of the Transport soldiers stepped to the still-open window and waved. "He's dead!" he bellowed. "Topo is dead!" Cheers, wails and renewed shooting greeted this announcement. Frank could smell smoke, laced with the unfamiliar tang of gunpowder and high explosives.

The other soldiers seized Frank and his father. "Damn it," old Rovzar snarled, "you apes had better—" One of the soldiers twisted the old man's arm, and the painter kicked him expertly, leaving him rolling in pain on the floor. Another raised his rifle clubwise.

"Duck, Dad!" yelled Frank, earning himself a slap in the side of the head.

His father had leaped away from the descending gun butt and made a grab at Costa's ruffle-bordered throat. One of the soldiers next to Frank stepped aside to have a clear field of fire. "*No!*" screamed Frank, twisting furiously in his captor's grasp. The soldier fired his rifle from the hip, almost casually, and the bang was startlingly loud. The bullet caught old Rovzar in the temple and spun him away from the surprised-looking prince. Frank, painfully held by two soldiers now, stared unbelievingly at his father's body stretched beside the bookcase.

"Take the kid along with the servants," said Costa, and as the soldiers, one of them limping and cursing, filed out, carrying Frank like a piece of furniture, the only coherent thought in Frank's stunned mind was that he was, if anything, somewhat older than Costa.

FRANK shifted now on his cot. The man who'd been having the nightmare seemed to have come to terms with his dreams, for the dark cells were silent except for the perpetual sussuration of many people breathing, a sound like water quietly flowing through pipes underground. We'd all better come to terms with our dreams, Frank thought. They'll be the best part of our lives, in the Orestes system.

No more painting, he thought, trying to make himself grasp the idea. No more friends, fencing, decent food and drink, girls—not ever again would he ride a horse through woods at dawn, not ever again swim in the surf, never again, in fact, feel the gravitational field of Octavio, the planet on which

he'd been born. Did you get sufficient use out of . . .
everything . . . while you still had it?

My God, he thought as the sudden sweat of com-
prehension misted his forehead and chilled his belly,
isn't there anyone who can get me *out* of this? What
about Tom Strand, or his father? Couldn't either of
them do anything? Of course not, rasped the logical
part of his mind. How could they reverse the decision
of the Transport and the planetary government? The
idea, he was forced to admit, was ridiculous.

Panic eventually gave way to a decision. I am *not*
going to Orestes, he thought. I simply am not going.
I *will* escape.

He got up from his cot and felt his way through the
inky blackness to one of the sleeping men and shook
him by the shoulder. The man started violently.

"Who is it?" he whispered in terror.

"I'm a fellow prisoner," Frank hissed. "Listen,
we've got to escape. Are you with me?"

"Oh, for God's sake, kid," the man almost sobbed,
"go back to sleep and leave me alone."

"You *want* to go to Orestes?" Frank asked
wonderingly.

"Kid—you can't escape. Forget it. Your life won't
be real great now, but make an escape attempt and
you'll be surprised how sorry you'll be, and for how
long."

Frank left the man to his sleep and returned to his
cot, his confident mood deflated.

After another half hour of sitting on his mattress,
Frank was again convinced of the necessity of escape. Wasn't there a wide ventilation grille set in
the center of the ceiling? He tried to remember. Let's
see, he thought, they marched us in here, showed
us each a cot, and then turned off the lights. But
it seems to me I did notice a slotted plate set in

the ceiling. I could escape through the ventilation system!

He stood up again. It seemed to be in the *center* of the ceiling, he recalled. He made his way to a wall and counted the number of steps it took to walk its length; then did the same with the other wall. Twelve by eight, he thought. He then went back to the midpoint of the twelve-pace wall and took four paces out into the room, thanking Chance that no sleeping prisoners lay in his path.

By my calculations, he mused, I should now be directly beneath that ventilation grille. He crouched; when he leaped upward with a strong kick, his fingers crooked to catch the vent. Instead, they cracked against unyielding concrete.

He fell back to the floor, strangling a curse. His hands stung, and he could feel blood trickling down one finger. Bit of a miscalculation, Rovzar, he told himself.

He pulled himself to his feet and got ready to jump again, this time only intending to brush the ceiling with his fingers, to feel for the vent. This is what I should have done to begin with, he thought.

After four jumps, muffled by his rubber-soled shoes, he found the vent. His next leap gained him two fingerholds and in a moment he had got a firm grip with both hands. Now what?

Why, he thought, I'll bring my legs up and kick the plate until it comes loose, and then I'll pull myself up into the hole and be off. Righto. He drew his legs up, and with a sort of half flip he kicked the plate with one toe. It made hardly any noise, but he was disappointed at how weak the blow was. This time he got swinging first, and then used the momentum of his pendulum motion to emphasize the kick as he flipped again and drove his heel at the grille.

With an echoing clang of broken metal his foot punched completely through the grille. The recoil of the kick wrenched his hands free, but he didn't fall back to the floor; instead he hung upside down, his foot caught in the twisted wreck of the vent.

Shouts echoed eerily through the corridors, and the prisoners below Frank whimpered in uncomprehending fear. An alarm added its flat howl to the confusion. Frank, dangling from the ceiling, pulled at his trapped foot, hoping to be able to return to his cot before the guards arrived. Footsteps thudded in the corridor, and immediately the lights in Frank's cell flashed on, blinding him. The will to move left his body and he relaxed, swinging limp from the mooring of his foot. He heard the door rattle and squeak open, and then something hard was driven with savage force into his stomach and consciousness left him.

FRANK came back to wakefulness by degrees, like a length of seaweed being gradually nudged to shore by succeeding waves. First he was aware of a hum of voices and a sense of being carried about. None of it seemed to demand a response.

Then he dimly knew he was sleeping, but it was a deep, heavy sleep, and he did not want to wake up yet even though it sounded as if some people were up already.

Abruptly, a cold finger and thumb pried his right eyelid open. Frank saw an unfocused sea of bright gray.

"This kid's okay," came a loud, gravelly voice. "Throw him over there with that clown who set his bed on fire."

Frank had groggily assumed that the voice was

speaking figuratively when it said "throw," but now
unseen hands clamped on his ankles and wrists. "Wait,
wait—" Frank began mumbling. "Heave *ho!*" called
someone cheerily, and Frank found himself lifted
from whatever he'd been lying on and tossed sprawling into the air. His eyes sprang open wide and he
grabbed convulsively at nothing. He saw the concrete
floor rushing up at him and he managed to twist
around in midair so that he landed on his hip instead
of his head. The sharp, aching pain of the impact was
his first clear sensation of the morning.

Laughter rang loud in the room, and Frank looked
up from where he lay to see what sort of people were
amused by this. A Transport captain and four guards
returned his gaze with a mixture of humor and scorn-
ful contempt in their eyes. All of them wore pistols,
and two of the guards held coils of rope.

"Take these two jerks first," said the captain,
pointing in Frank's direction. "And tie their hands."
The man exited and the four guards walked over to
Frank and rolled him over onto his face, then quickly
and securely tied his wrists together behind him.
They left him lying there and moved on to someone
behind him.

"Get up now," one of the guards said. Frank
struggled to his knees and then stood up. His stomach was a collage of pain and numbness, and he
sagged when he straightened up; the colors of uncon-
sciousness began to glitter before his eyes. He lowered his head and breathed deeply, and the weakness
passed. He heard a sigh behind him and turned to see
a tall, thin man with graying hair. It must be the guy
who set fire to his bed, Frank realized.

"All right, you two, get moving," a guard said.
"Out that door."

Frank and his sad-eyed companion shambled out

of the little room and, escorted by the guards, made their way down a corridor to an open doorway. Morning sunlight glared on wet asphalt outside, and the air was cold.

Somehow Frank was not very depressed. The light of day had dispelled the fears of the night, and his system was buoyed up by the realization that he was embarking on a perilous journey. Anything can happen, he thought.

The guards prodded the two blinking prisoners outside. Five hundred yards away the silver needle of a Transport ship stood up against the sky, gleaming in the sun like a polished sword. Even though it was the vehicle that was to carry him to Orestes, Frank was overcome with the beauty of the thing.

"Are these our two escapees?" asked a Transport officer who had walked up while Frank was staring at the rocket. He carried in his hand an object that looked like a rubber stamp or a wax seal.

"Yes, sir," answered one of the guards.

"Open their shirts," the officer said. A guard took hold of Frank's shirt-collar ends and yanked them apart. Three buttons clicked on the asphalt. I'm glad this is just an old painting shirt, Frank thought automatically. He heard his companion's shirt being dealt with in the same way.

"Now, boys, this won't hurt a bit," said the officer with a cold smile as he pressed the seal onto Frank's chest. The metal felt warm and itched a little, but was not uncomfortable. "There," the officer said. "Now everyone will know at a glance who you are."

Frank looked down past his chin and saw a mark on his chest. It was a circle with a capital E inside it. "Escapee," the officer explained. He turned to the guards. "Get these monkeys aboard. We lift at nine-seventeen." He strode off without another word.

"You heard the man, lads," grinned a guard. "Start walking. Your friends will be coming along as soon as you two maniacs are aboard." Flanked by the arrogant guards, Frank and the bed-burner set off across the tarmac toward the ship. Frank's eyes were becoming accustomed to the daylight and he looked around as he walked. To his right, a hundred yards away, was a chain-link fence topped with strands of barbed wire. Half-a-dozen big tractor motors were stacked against it at one point. Beyond the fence, he knew, was the channel in which the Malachi River surged its way to the distant sea. At his left was visible a cluster of undistinguished gray buildings. Not a really fine view, Frank thought, considering it's probably the last time I'll see this planet. The thought raised a clamoring flock of emotions in him, which he determinedly strangled and put away. It simply would not do, he told himself, to burst into tears out here.

The gray-haired prisoner who paced along beside Frank was acting oddly. He was whimpering, and his wide-open eyes flicked around as if he were watching the quick, erratic course of a wasp. "Are you okay?" asked Frank quietly.

"There's no way," the man said.

"What's that?" asked a guard.

"There's no way!" the man shouted. The guards, sensing a dangerous frenzy, backed away a pace. Frank did, too. The guards were all concentrating their attention on the crazed bed-burner, and it occurred to Frank that since Francisco Rovzar was already branded as an escapee, he had nothing to lose by trying it again. He took another step back, so that the guards were all in front of him.

"Oh my God, there's no way!" shrieked the gray-haired man, who now took off at a dead run toward the buildings. At the same moment Frank turned and sprinted, as quietly as he could, toward the chain-link fence and the tractor motors. He heard, without thinking about it, angry calls behind him. Forget it, he thought, they're after that old guy. Keep running.

"Hey, *you!*" sounded an exasperated shout. That's probably me he's yelling at; well, I have to play out the hand now, he thought. He strained for more speed, ignoring the shortness of his breath and the pain in his stomach. The fence seemed to slowly jerk closer. Vividly, he pictured the guard unsnapping the flap on his holster, lifting out the pistol, and raising it to eye level. Should I weave right and left to spoil their aim? No, that'd slow me down, he thought.

"Hold it right there, kid, or I'll shoot," called one of the guards. Frank covered the last ten feet and leaped, arms still bound, to the oily top of one of the tractor motors; without stopping he sprang up the stairs they formed, and then jumped with all his strength to clear the barbed wire. A gunshot cracked and his body jerked as it fell away, awkwardly, on the other side of the fence.

"You get him?" asked one of the guards.

"Sure I got him," the other guard replied, holstering his gun.

"A lucky shot at this range. You must have aimed high," commented another. "I'll send the grounds patrol to pick up the body. Come on, help me get this guy stowed." The guards picked up the unconscious, bleeding form of the unfortunate bed-burner and strode off toward the ship.

Chapter 3

Frank's flying leap ended in a ragged slide down a dirt embankment to a service road below. The breath was knocked out of him, and the side of his head stung where the bullet had creased him. He lay still for a minute or two to get his breath back, but he knew he couldn't rest yet. He struggled to his skinned knees and spit dirt out of his mouth. I've *got* to untie my hands, he realized, looking around desperately for some object with a sharp edge. He saw nothing but the hill and the road.

He got shakily to his feet, but didn't feel able to walk. Blood from his right ear ran down his neck and stained his ruined shirt. I can't take a whole lot more of this, he thought. Looking south, away from the slope, he could see the steep banks of the Malachi. That's where I want to go, he told himself. The Malachi flows right into Munson, and that ancient metropolis has been harboring fugitives for five hundred years.

The grating roar of a jeep interrupted his thoughts. He knew there was no place to hide, so he flopped down on his stomach beside the road, lying on his good ear. A few moments later the jeep rounded the corner and bore down on his lifeless-looking body. It squealed to a halt beside him, its motor still chugging. Frank held his breath.

"Look at him," remarked the driver. "The bullet went right through his head."

"Lemme see," spoke up his partner. "Wow. I wish they'd issue guns to us."

"Hah," replied the driver. "Like to see you try to handle a gun."

"I could do it."

"Yeah, sure. Throw our friend here into the back, will you?"

"Aren't you gonna give me a hand?"

"No, I've got to stay here and keep my foot on the clutch. Hurry up."

"Oh, man," whined the other, climbing out of the vehicle. Frank heard his boots crunch in the dirt as the man walked over to his prostrate form. Rough hands grabbed his shoulders and pulled. I can't keep playing dead, Frank thought, terrified; I *can't*. Any second now they're going to notice.

"This guy's *heavy*," the man complained.

"For God's sake, Howard, he's skinny. Now stop bitching and toss him in here."

Howard lifted Frank by the belt and slipped an arm under his stomach. Then with an exaggerated groan he heaved the limp body up onto his shoulder. Frank managed to keep from tensing any muscles during the maneuver, but couldn't help opening his eyes as Howard flung him into the back of the jeep. There was a spare tire, and he bent a little to let his head land on the rubber; a jack jabbed painfully into his shoulder, but he found himself basically uninjured. He was very tempted to give himself up. I've taken as much as anyone could have expected of me, he thought. All I want is a little rest.

With the lurching rattle of engaging gears the jeep got underway. Frank lay face up on the spare tire, his right foot only a short distance from the back of the driver's head. The machine picked up speed, and the driver clanked the stick shift into second gear; after a couple of minutes he pushed it up into third.

Frank risked raising his head. The road took a sharp curve to the left in front of them, and the driver's hand reached out to downshift. Without stopping to think, Frank drew his right leg all the way back and slammed his foot like a piston into the base of the driver's skull. The man's head bounced off the steering wheel and the jeep spun to the right in a bucking dry skid. Off balance from his kick, Frank was pitched over the jeep's side panel; he hit the dirt in a sitting position and slid, taking most of the abrasion on his left thigh and shoulder. When he found himself motionless at last, he decided to die there, right there in the road. I should have died a long time ago, he thought.

He cautiously opened his eyes. The jeep lay on its side a hundred feet away—the tires on the top side were still spinning, and the motor was ticking in a staccato rattle. Frank was about to close his eyes again when he noticed a jagged strip of the hood protruding like a knife. Squinting against dizziness, he got to his feet after overcoming a short spasm in one knee that had him genuflecting like a madman. He limped across the road to the jeep, and backed up against the torn piece of metal, rocking back and forth to saw through the rope binding him. The rhythm of the motion brought to his dazed mind the memory of a song his father used to sing, and after a brief time of rocking in the morning sun he began to sing it:

> "I open my study window
> And into the twilight peer,
> And my anxious eyes are watching
> For the man with my evening beer."

The rope frayed, then snapped, and Frank's hands were free at last. He flexed them to get the blood circulating.

"Who's singing?" came an angry voice. Howard, his shirt torn, lurched around the corner of the up-ended jeep. His service sword, a short rapier, was drawn. Frank ran around the other side, and saw the driver's body lifeless in the road, face down with his knees drawn up like a supplicant in church. Frank hobbled over to the body and drew the sword from the scabbard on the dead man's belt. Its hilt was a right-handed one, but Frank held it in his left, trying to grip it with his skinned thumb and forefinger as Mr. Strand had taught him. Awkward, he thought. How good is Howard?

Howard came out from behind the barrier of the jeep; he was running at Frank, his sword held straight out before him like the horn of a charging rhinoceros. Frank parried it, but Howard had lumbered past before Frank could riposte. The big guard turned and aimed a slash at his young opponent's head; Frank ducked the blow and jabbed Howard in the right elbow.

"Damn!" Howard exploded. "Want to mess around, eh? Swallow this!" He jumped forward, thrusting at Frank's stomach. Frank, who had been through this move a hundred times in the fencing academy, parried the sword down and outward in seconde, flipped his own sword back in line and lunged at Howard's chest. The point entered just beneath the breastbone, and Howard's forward impetus drove the blade into the heart. Frank watched, both horrified and fascinated, as Howard sagged and slid away from the streaked blade that had transfixed him. His body went to its knees and then fell forward into the dust of the road.

Frank backed away. Old Strand was right, he realized; hardly anybody can really fence. Since guns were rapidly becoming unavailable, the sword was coming back into fashion, but there had not yet been time for fencing strategy to become widely known.

A breath of wind stirred Frank's hair. I can't rest quite yet, he realized. I've got to get down to the Malachi. He half-climbed, half-slid down the embankment on the south side of the road. His ear had stopped bleeding and only throbbed now, but his scraped knees and legs shot pain at him every time he bent them. It was an annoying pain, and it roused in him a powerful anger against the self-righteous Transports who had done this to him. And who killed your father, he reminded himself.

He swore that if the opportunity ever presented itself, he would take revenge against the Transports and Duke Costa.

He soon came to level ground—an expanse of slick clay soil, littered with rocks and thriving shrubs. He crossed this quickly and found himself standing at the top of a forty-foot cliff; below him, through a bed of white sand, flowed the green water of the Malachi. During the summer the river was a leisurely, curling stream, knotted with oxbows, but it was a spring breeze that now plucked at Frank's tattered clothes, and the river was young and quick.

The painstaking labor of ten minutes got him to the bottom of the cliff. After diving into the cool water and incautiously drinking a quantity of it, he set about looking for objects on which to float downstream. He found two warped wooden doors dumped behind a clump of bushes and decided to use these, one on top of the other, as a raft. If he sat up on it, he discovered, his raft had a tendency to flip over; but a passenger lying down had no difficulties. He tore a wide frond from one of the dwarf palm trees that abounded and used it to shade his face from the midmorning sun. Soon he was moving along with the current, and when he remembered Howard's rapier it was too late to turn back to retrieve the weapon. He shrugged at the loss and drifted on, warmed by the sun above him, cooled by the water below, shaded by his palm frond, sleeping the sleep of exhaustion.

THUS he drifted east, through the Madstone Marshes, under the towering marble spans of the Cromlech Bridge, and through miles of forests. Any eyes that may have spied the makeshift raft felt that neither it nor its passenger were worth bothering. By midafternoon the walls and towers of Munson rose massive ahead.

At the western boundary of Munson, the Malachi divided in two; the first channel, its natural one, took it under the carved bridges and around the gondola docks, across the sandy delta to the Deptford Sea, sometimes called the Eastern Sea. The other channel, built two centuries previously by Duke Giroud, entered a great arched tunnel and passed underground, beneath the southern section of the city, to facilitate the disposal of sewage. The city had declined since Giroud's day, and most of the sewers were no longer in use, but the southern branch of the Malachi River, the branch called the Leethee by the citizens, still flowed under Munson's streets.

Frank was still asleep when he drifted near the ancient gothic masonry of Munson's high walls. Two arches loomed before him, foam splashing between them where the waters parted. The great walls with their flying buttresses dwarfed even the couriers' carracks that sometimes passed this way, and none of the river scavengers of the west end noticed as an unwieldy bit of rectangular debris hesitated, rocked in the swirl, and then drifted through the Leethee arch and slid down into the darkness beyond.

BEARDO Jackson tamped his clay pipe and sucked at it with relish, blowing clouds of smoke up at the stones of the ceiling. Below him in the darkness the waters of one of the many branches of the Leethee could be heard gurgling and slapping against the brickwork, washing in a dark tide below the cellars of the city.

He struck another match and held it to the wick of a rusty lantern beside him. A bright yellow flame sprang up, illuminating the cavernlike chamber in which Beardo sat perched on a swaying bridge. The light flickered over the walls of tight-fitted stones reinforced with timber in many places; the arched tunnel-openings that gaped at either end of the bridge remained in deep shadow.

"Morgan!" Beardo called. "Come along, the tide's high!" His voice echoed weirdly, receding up the watercourse until it reverberated like a distant chorus of operatic frogs.

A woman appeared at the opening on Beardo's right. She carried a coil of fifty-pound fishing line;

before stepping out onto the bridge, she looped one end of it around an iron hook imbedded in the wall.

"Don't yell like that," she said. "You never know who might be around."

"Oh, to hell with that," he sneered. "Everybody within a cubic mile of here is scared stiff of me." He slapped the sheathed knife at his belt and laughed in what he believed was a sinister fashion. The woman spat over the rope rail and stepped out onto the bridge. She was sloppily fat, and the bridge creaked and quivered as it took her weight.

"Easy, woman," Beardo said. "The bridge was built for frailer girls." He grinned up at her. The whites of his eyes were almost brown, and his face, loosely draped over the bones of his skull, was as wrinkled and creased as a long-unchanged bedsheet. His beard was ragged and patchy, as were his clothes.

"And what would frailer girls be doing on it?" she asked scornfully. Beardo rolled his eyes and made lascivious motions with his hands, implying that there were any number of things frail girls might do on it.

"You rotten toad," Morgan snarled, slapping the old man affectionately in the side of the head.

"We've no time for fooling around," Beardo declared. "Where's the hooks?"

Morgan pulled a chain of small grappling hooks from a bag at her belt, and proceeded to tie one of them to the fishing line. She tossed it into the water so that it trailed downstream.

"Okay now, keep your eyes open on this side, so we'll know where to swing the line," Beardo said, facing upstream. "If anything *scares* you, just call me," he added sarcastically. A week ago a dead lion had floated by under the bridge—its hide would have made a fine catch, but Morgan, terrified by the glazed

feline eyes, had twitched the trailing hook away from
it. Beardo had not yet entirely forgiven her for it.

"Oh, bite a crawdad," she said.

They were silent then, staring intently into the
lamplit water. Beardo and his woman were, in the
understreet slang, "working the shores": scavenging
the debris the Leethee brought in from the upper
world. Many of the understreet population of Munson
made a profitable living at this trade.

Suddenly Beardo stiffened; something was drifting
downstream, something that bumped frequently against
the brick walls. "Look sharp, girl," he whispered.
"Sounds like a piece of wood coming along."

Presently the thing was dimly visible. "It's a midget
raft! With a guy on it!" whispered Morgan. Beardo
poked her with his elbow to shut her up. The raft,
which was indeed a notably small one, rocked forward into the light. Morgan gasped when she saw the
passenger, for its head appeared to be a cluster of
rigid green tentacles.

"Beelzebub!" she cried.

The figure sat up on the raft abruptly, making
hooting sounds. Morgan screamed. The tiny craft
flipped over, dumping its rider into the cold black
water.

Beardo, who had seen the palm frond fall away,
and knew that this underground mariner was only a
puzzled-looking young man, slithered under the rope
bridge-rail and dropped into the water ten feet below.
He caught the floundering intruder and pushed him
toward the ladder rungs set in the brick wall. The
young man caught the rungs and began to haul himself out of the bad-smelling tide. His black hair was
down across his face, and he stared up through it
with bloodshot eyes. Morgan wailed and scrambled

on all fours off of the bridge; she disappeared into one of the tunnel mouths, still wailing.

The dark-haired youth pulled himself up onto the bridge and sat there shivering. Beardo climbed up right behind and sat down beside him. The old scavenger smiled, pulled out a long knife and began cleaning his hideous fingernails.

"And what might they call you at home, lad?" Beardo queried.

"What?"

"What's your name?"

"Francisco Rovzar. Uh, Frank . . . what's yours?" asked the young man.

"Puddin' Tame," answered Beardo gleefully. "Ask me again and I'll tell you the same." The old man giggled like a manic parrot, slapping his thigh with his free hand.

"Where is this?" asked Frank. "Am I in Munson?"

"Oh aye," nodded Beardo. "Or *under* it, to be more precise. What port was it you sailed from, sir?"

"I've been drifting east on the Malachi from the Barclay Transport Depot." Frank wished the old man would put away the knife. He didn't like the look or smell of the ancient stone watercourse, and he wondered just how far under Munson he was.

"Barclay, eh? You a jailbird?"

Frank considered lying, but this old creature didn't look like he had police connections; and Frank desperately needed friends and food and safe lodging. It's almost certainly an error to trust this guy, he thought. But the next one I meet could be a lot worse.

"Yes," he answered. "That is, I was a prisoner until about eight this morning."

"Released you, did they?"

"No. I escaped."

Beardo started to laugh derisively, then noticed Frank's scrapes and bruises and ruined ear. "You *did*?" he asked, surprised. "Well, you don't often hear of *that* being done. Anyway, Frank, what I really want to . . . uh . . . *ascertain*, is whether or not you have a family that would be willing to pay an old gentleman like myself for your safe return. Do you understand?"

"No," said Frank.

"Ransom, Frank, ransom. Do you have a rich family?" Before Frank could think of a safe answer, Beardo answered himself. "No, I suppose you don't. If you did, they would have bought you out of Barclay. Or maybe the whole family got arrested, hmm?"

Frank shook his head. "No family at all," he said hopelessly. "My father was all I had, and the Transports shot him yesterday."

"Ah!" said Beardo sadly, testing his knife's edge with a discolored thumb. "I'm afraid that narrows down the possibilities for you, Frank my boy."

Do I have the strength to fight old Puddin' Tame? Frank asked himself. I don't think I do. Maybe I could get into the water again.

"Your father and you were thieves, I take it?" Beardo asked, squinting speculatively at Frank's bared throat.

"No!" Frank exclaimed, stung now in his much abused pride. "My father is . . . was Claude M. Rovzar, the best portrait painter on this planet."

Beardo blinked. He was inclined to doubt this, but then saw the paint stains on the ragged remains of the youth's shirt.

"You're full of surprises, Frank," he said. "All right, let's say you *are* Rovzar's son. Why would the Transports shoot Claude Rovzar?"

"My father was doing a portrait of Duke Topo yesterday. Transport troops invaded the palace. Costa was with them, and he killed the old Duke. The Transports grabbed my father and me, and my father resisted. They shot him."

"You keep saying they shot him. You don't mean that literally, do you?"

"Yes. There was more gunfire yesterday than I've ever heard of, anywhere, in a hundred years. Bombs, even."

"Hmm," grunted Beardo, scratching his furry chin. "There just might be something to all this." He stood up, setting the bridge swaying. "One thing, anyway," he said, "you've earned a reprieve." He slapped his knife back into its sheath. "Come with me. We'll get your wounds cleaned up and feed you. Then you can tell your story to a friend of mine."

Beardo picked up his lantern and Frank followed him into one of the tunnels.

Chapter 4

Alarmingly, the tunnel Beardo and Frank followed led *down*. The dim, shifty light cast by the old man's lantern did little to dispel the darkness, and several times Frank heard anonymous scrabbling, splashing and low moans echo out of side corridors. Beardo held his drawn knife in his right hand and tapped it against the damp brick walls as he led Frank along.

"Why are you doing that?" Frank whispered.

"It shows any hole-lurkers that we're armed. Got to let 'em know we mean business."

Good God, Frank thought. I wonder what sort of creatures lurk in these holes. In spite of himself, Frank began thinking of tentacles and green, fanged faces under old slouch hats.

"Good sirs! Good sirs!" came a wheezing voice from the blackness ahead, causing Frank to start violently. "A penny to see a dancing dog?"

"No," rasped Beardo, advancing on the voice. "We don't want to see a dancing dog."

40

Frank peered ahead over Beardo's shoulder and saw an old person of indeterminate sex, as withered and dark as a dried apple. The figure was slumped against the wall as though it had been thrown there, but one upraised skeletal hand held crossed sticks from which dangled a malodorous puppet. Frank looked more closely at it and saw that it was the dried corpse of a dog.

"Just keep walking," whispered Beardo to Frank. "I've seen this one before."

The old puppeteer began to sing, and Frank knew it was a woman. "Tirra lee, tirra lee, dance hound," she crooned, and jiggled the horrible puppet merrily. Beardo stepped around her, smiling ingratiatingly. Frank followed, also attempting to smile.

"Beardo, by the stars!" the old woman exclaimed. "You'll give me some money, now, eh?"

"Certainly, soon as I get some," replied the old man, walking on down the tunnel and pulling Frank by the wrist.

"Soon as you *get* some? Damn your treacherous eyes!" the woman brayed. She struggled to her feet and stumbled after them for a few paces, flailing Frank's back with her mummified dog, before sinking exhausted to the flagstones once more. "A penny to see a dancing dog?" she inquired of the darkness.

BEARDO'S home was an abandoned section of a spiral stairwell, left over from God-knew-what derelict subway system. The old man hung his lantern on a wall peg and touched a match to three kerosene lamps; the comparatively bright light enabled Frank to see the place in some detail. The shaft was roughly twenty-five feet from stone floor to boarded-up roof, and the ascending iron stairs circled the shaft twice before disappearing beyond the boards of the ceiling. Stacks of books, chipped statues, rusted ironmongery and clothes lined the outer edges of the stairs, with the other half, near the wall, left clear for ascending and descending. In the middle of the floor was a sunken tub in whose murky waters several large toads sported.

"Well, Frankie lad, what think you of the old homestead, eh?" asked Beardo, unscrewing the lid of a coffee jar.

Even in his cold, wet state, Frank could see that Beardo fairly radiated the homeowner's pride, so he answered tactfully. "It's beautiful, Mr. Tame. A regular palace. I didn't know underground homes were so . . . roomy."

"Hardly any of them are, Frank. This is one of the finest dwellings, I believe, in all of Munson Understreet. Oh, and my name is Beardo, Beardo Jackson; that Puddin' Tame business was a joke." The old man put a pan of water over a gas flame, and then turned to Frank, "Well now, off with those old rags and hop in the tub."

"The tub? But . . . there's frogs in the tub."

"Toads. They thrive on the warm water. No poisonous frogs in my home. Hop in."

Come on, Frank told himself. This tub is the least of your worries. He undraped the tatters of cloth from his shivering body and lowered himself gingerly into the tub, which actually was warm. He splashed around for a while with the toads and then crawled out, feeling, to his surprise, considerably better for the bath. The old man dressed and bandaged Frank's bullet-torn right ear.

Beardo had selected clothes to replace his ruined ones and had not spared the finery. Frank donned a pair of purple silk trousers, red leather shoes, and a black shirt with pearl buttons. Over all went a white quilted smoking jacket with tassels and embroidered dragons.

"How do I look?" Frank asked.

"Like a prince. Come on, down this coffee and we'll be off to visit Mr. Orcrist."

SAM ORCRIST liked to think of himself as a ruler-in-the-shadows, a confidant of kings, a prompter behind the scenes. He was privy to the secrets of almost everyone, and his unstable fortune was spread about in hundreds of obscure and fabulous investments. Pages in the Ducal Palace left reports for him in certain unused sewer grates; ladies at court passed on to him incriminating letters through waiters and footmen; and children, above and below the streets, were sent by his agents on all sorts of furtive tracking-and-finding missions.

Orcrist entertained often, but selectively. The doors of his understreet apartment were closed to some of the most influential citizens on the planet, and warmly open to a few of the most unsavory.

"Mr. Beardo Jackson and a young man wish to see you, sir," said Orcrist's doorman, standing beside the chair in which Orcrist sat reading a book of Keats.

"Well don't leave them standing out there for the footpads, Pons. Show them in." He closed his book and took a bottle and three glasses out of a cabinet. He was pouring the liquor when Beardo and Frank entered.

"Beardo!" he said. "Good to see you again. What have you been doing to throw Morgan into a hysterical fright?"

"Good evening, Sam," Beardo replied. "Poor old Morgan mistook my young friend here for an archfiend."

"I see. Who is your young friend?"

"He's Frank Rovzar, the son of Claude Rovzar the painter. And he has an interesting and timely story to tell you. Frank, sit down and tell Sam what happened yesterday."

Comfortable in his new clothes and warmed by Orcrist's brandy, Frank told him about the rebellion at the palace and the deaths of his father and Duke Topo.

"Holy smokes," said Orcrist when Frank finished. "And you're sure it was Transport troops that took the palace?"

"Yes," Frank answered. "Led by Prince Costa."

"I *wondered* why there's been no news from the palace in the last twenty-four hours. They're certainly keeping the lid on this." He stood up. "Pons!"

"Yes sir?" answered the doorman.

"Get up to the land office *fast*, and sell all my holdings in the Goriot Valley. Don't start a run on it, but be willing to take a loss. And for God's sake get there before the office closes. Go!" Pons dashed from the room. "Don't come back until I no longer own one square foot of farmland!" Orcrist called after him.

He strode to the table and drummed his fingers on its polished surface. "How old is this news, Beardo?" he asked.

"I pulled Frank out of the water less than an hour ago."

"Excellent. To show my gratitude for your prompt action, Beardo, I insist that Mr. Rovzar and yourself consent to be my guests for dinner. You'll sleep here, of course; I'll have Pons show you your rooms when he returns."

Frank was beginning to feel dizzy, and doubtful of his own perceptions. Whatever response he had expected Orcrist to have to his story, this had not been it.

"What's the connection," Frank asked, "between a rebellion at the palace and farmland in the Goriot Valley?"

Orcrist smiled, not unkindly. "I'm sorry if I seem callous about all this," he said. "I'm an investor, you see. About ten years ago Duke Topo, in an attempt to make Octavio an autonomous—that is, self-sufficient—planet, planted and irrigated the entire length of the Goriot Valley. That way we didn't have to import produce. It was a flourishing undertaking, and I am at this moment the owner of much of that farmland. But if the Transport has taken control of us, I don't want any part of that damned valley. The Transport doesn't approve of independent planets, and I don't see a bright future for agriculture on Octavio." He tossed off the last of his drink. "And now if you'll excuse me, I have a few other little matters to take care of."

With a stately bow, Orcrist left the room. Beardo crossed to the table and refilled his glass. "A real gentleman!" he smiled, luxuriously sniffing his brandy.

"He certainly is," agreed Frank, to whom, right now, the word "dinner" was like a loved one's name. "It was nice of him to ask us to stay the night here," he added, wondering where he would have slept in Beardo's odd dwelling.

"Ah, well that wasn't so much good manners as *caution*, you see," Beardo said. "Any time someone brings him really hot news he insists that they remain here until the news isn't hot anymore. He doesn't want us telling your story to anyone else." The old fellow sipped the brandy and pulled out his pipe. "And his hospitality, Frankie, is such that no one has ever been known to object to the temporary captivity."

The dinner, which was served an hour later in
Orcrist's high-ceilinged dining room, was lavish. A
dozen stuffed game hens were piled on a platter in
the center of the table, and salads, baked potatoes,
toast, cold meats and steaming sauces flanked them.
Carafes of chilled wines stood next to the roasted
hens; Frank was amazed to find out that the whole
production was intended only for himself, Beardo,
Orcrist, and one other house-bound guest.

"Frank Rovzar, Beardo Jackson, this is George
Tyler," said Orcrist as the four of them sat down at
the table. "George, Frank and Beardo."

Frank looked across a dish of mustard sauce at
George Tyler. He looks like he drinks more than he
ought to, Frank thought, though he's still too young
for it to really show. Oblivious to Frank's scrutiny,
Tyler brushed a lock of blond hair out of his face
and speared a baked potato.

"I must request, friends, that you do not discuss
the respective businesses that have brought you here,"
said Orcrist. "Not that any of it would provide suitable dinner conversation anyway."

He took a long sip of wine, holding it in his mouth
to warm it and taste it before he swallowed. "Not
bad," he decided. "You and Frank should get along
well, George," he said. "You have the artistic tem-
perament in common. Frank is a painter, and George,"
he added, turning to Frank, "is a poet." The two
young men smiled at each other embarrassedly.

"To hell with the talk, I say," put in Beardo,
gnawing a greasy hen from whose open abdomen
pearl onions cascaded onto his plate. "Mother of
God!" he exclaimed, observing the phenomenon.

The dinner progressed with considerable gusto,
and by ten o'clock most of the wine and food had
disappeared. Frank was feeling powerfully sleepy,

though the others seemed to be just blooming, and Beardo had begun singing vulgar songs.

Tyler tossed a clean-picked bone onto his plate. "Not bad fare, Sam," he said. "Nearly as good as what they used to serve at the palace."

"At the palace?" inquired Frank politely.

"Oh, yes," Tyler nodded, a little clumsily. "Didn't old Sam tell you? I'm the eldest son of Topo."

Orcrist caught Frank's eye and frowned warningly. Don't worry, Frank thought, I won't say anything.

"Oh, hell yes," Tyler went on. "Many's the morning Dad and I would go hunting deer with the game wardens. I had my own horse, naturally, a speckled roan named . . . uh . . . Lighthoof." He drank the last of his wine and refilled his glass. "Oh, and the long evenings on the seaside terrace, the sunset light reflecting in our drinking cups carved of single emeralds! Sitting in our adjustable recliners, fanned by tall, silent slaves from the lands where the bong trees grow!"

"For God's sake, George," said Orcrist.

"Oh, I know, Sam," Tyler said with a broad wave of his hand. "I shouldn't . . . dwell on these things now that I move in lower circles . . . present company excluded, of course. But I long even now for that old life, to mount old . . . Lightboy and ride off on adventures and quests and whatnot."

At this point Frank slumped forward onto the tablecloth, fast asleep.

FRANK opened his eyes, but closed them again when he saw that the room was in pitch blackness. Not dawn yet, he thought. I wonder if Dad is home. A raucous, choking snore from another room made him sit up, completely awake. That's not Dad, he thought; and this isn't my room. Where am I? He felt around

on the top of the table beside the bed, and soon had
struck a match to a candle.

I'm in one of Orcrist's guest rooms, he realized.
And we're underground, so God knows what time it
is. He got out of bed and found his gaudy clothes
draped over a chair. Odd as they were, he felt better
when he was dressed. Now then, he thought. What
are Orcrist's breakfast customs?

He sighted the door, and then snuffed the candle
and groped to it in the dark. To his relief the silent
hallway beyond was lit by wall cressets, and he
wandered along it until he came to Orcrist's sitting
room.

"Ah, Frank," said Orcrist, who sat in an easy
chair with a book and a cup of coffee. "Up with the
sun even down here, eh? As a matter of fact, I've
been waiting for you." He stood up and took two
rolls of parchment out from behind a bust of Byron
on one of his bookshelves. Then he unrolled them on
the carpet, using books to hold the corners down.
On one of them had been done a finely shaded
drawing of a girl's head; the other was blank.

"What do you think of that picture, Frank?" Orcrist
asked.

"I'd say it's one of Gascoyne's best sketches of
Dora Wakefield. People used to say he was having
an affair with her, but my father never believed it."

Orcrist blinked. "Well, you know your field, Frank,
that's certain. Yes, it is a Gascoyne, though I didn't
know the name of the model. What I want to know is
whether you can, without compromising any princi-
ples, *copy* it for me on this blank sheet. Hm?"

"Sure I can," Frank answered carelessly. "Have
you got black ink, a little water, and a . . . number
eight point pen?"

Orcrist pointed to them on the bookcase. "I'll be

back in an hour to get you for breakfast," he said, and left the room, carrying his coffee.

Frank rubbed the sleep out of his eyes and got to work. He lightly sketched the face onto the blank sheet using a dry pen to lay down some guide-scratches; then he dipped the pen in the ink and began carefully mimicking Gascoyne's delicate stippling and cross-hatching. The discipline of his craft took his mind off of the uncertainty of his current situation. Except for the occasional clink of pen-nib against ink bottle, the room was silent.

When Orcrist returned, he found Frank sitting in the easy chair, reading.

"Given up?" he asked with a little annoyance.

Frank handed him the two rolls of parchment. "Which one is Gascoyne's?" he asked. Orcrist unrolled one, looked at it, and replaced it on the table. He unrolled the other one more carelessly, stared at it closely, and then spread both of them out on the floor.

"Given up?" asked Frank.

Abruptly, Orcrist laughed. "Yes, by God," he said. "Which is yours?"

"The one whose ear lobe is showing. I didn't want to do an absolute copy."

Orcrist laughed again and clapped Frank on the shoulder. "Come along to breakfast," he said. "And we can discuss your career possibilities."

Chapter 5

Beardo was staring with ill-concealed distaste at a glistening fried egg on his plate. With a petulant jab of his fork he ripped open the yolk.

"There's a sad sight for you, poet," he said somberly.

"Oh, quit playing with it," said Tyler.

Both of them were frowning and squinting, and they seemed to have occasional trouble in breathing.

"Beardo," said Orcrist, leading Frank into the breakfast room, which was cheerily lit by actual sunlight reflected down a shaft from the surface. "Your boy here proves to be a competent art forger. I propose to buy him from you. How does sixty malories sound?"

"You're too generous, I'm sure," smiled Beardo, cheered by this unexpected windfall. "Sixty it is."

Frank was surprised to find that he was a buyable article, but he said nothing.

"How do you feel about that, Frank?" asked Orcrist.

"You'd be a licensed art forger, bonded to me. You can have room and board here, plus a good salary, half of which, for the first two years, goes to me. Then when your bond is paid off you keep all of it. Will you take it?"

How can I not take it, Frank thought. It sounds like a good deal, and there's absolutely nothing else I can do. He bowed. "I'd be delighted, Mr. Orcrist. Where do I sign?"

"After breakfast, can't do business before breakfast. Why, gentlemen, you've eaten nothing! Not hungry?" He winked at Frank. Beardo and Tyler shook their heads.

"Well I thank you for your company anyway. I assume two such busy citizens as yourselves must have many appointments, so I won't inconvenience you by insisting that you stay for lunch."

ORCRIST told Frank that they'd get him registered with the Subterranean Companions that night. In honor of the occasion he provided Frank with some clothes of a more sober nature: a suit of brown corduroy, black boots and a black overcoat. "It's not a good idea to be too conspicuous down here," he confided. "If you went out dressed in those other clothes, the first thief who saw you would figure it was Ali Baba himself walking by, and bash you before you could blink."

Frank examined the conservative lines of his new overcoat with some relief. "Who are the Subterranean Companions?" he asked.

"A brotherhood of laborers engaged in extralegal work. A thieves' union, actually. And we've got to get your name on the roll. Freelance work simply isn't permitted."

"Well, I want to do this right," Frank put in.

"Of course you do."

That evening, after a much simpler dinner than the previous night's, Orcrist and Frank set off down Sheol Boulevard, a grand street whose brick roof stood a full twenty feet above the cobblestones. Streetlamps were hung from chains at intervals of roughly fifteen paces, and taverns, fuel stores and barber shops cast light through their open doorways onto the pavement.

"This, I guess you could say, is Downtown Understreet," said Orcrist. "Three blocks farther are the good restaurants. We've even got a couple of good bookstores down here."

"Will we be passing them?" asked Frank.

"Not tonight. We've got to turn south on Bolt after this next cross street."

They walked on without speaking, listening to the sounds of the understreet metropolis—laughter, shouts, clanking dishes and lively accordion music—echoing up and down the dim avenues.

At Bolt Street they turned right, and then took a sharp jog left, into an alleymouth, and stopped. They were in almost total darkness.

"Where are we?" whispered Frank.

"Sh!"

He heard the rattle of keys, and then the scratch and snap of a lock turning. Orcrist's hand closed on his shoulder and guided him forward a few paces. There was a breath of air, and the sound of the lock again, and then a match flared in the blackness and Orcrist was holding it to the wick of a small pocket lantern. The narrow hallway smelled of old french fries. Orcrist put his finger to his lips and led Frank forward, past several similar doors, to a stairway.

"Going down," Orcrist whispered.

At the bottom of the stairs, six flights down, Orcrist

relaxed and began chatting. "Got to be careful, you see, Frank," he said. "There are people who'd pay a lot for the death of a ranking member of the Companions, so I never come by the same route twice in a row." They were walking along another corridor now, but it was brighter and wider, and Orcrist extinguished his lantern and put it away.

"Why aren't you armed?" asked Frank, who had noticed the absence of a sword under Orcrist's cape.

"Oh, I'm adequately armed, never fear. Ah, and here we are."

They stepped through a high open arch into a huge hall that Frank thought must once have been a church. The pews, if it ever did have any, had been ripped out and replaced by ranks of folding wooden chairs, but the place was still lit by eight ancient baroque chandeliers. A big, altarlike block of marble up front was currently being used as a speaker's platform.

Frank followed Orcrist up a ramp to an overhanging structure that might have been a side-wall choir loft or a theater box. "Make yourself at home," Orcrist told him, gesturing at the dusty chairs and music stands that littered the box. "I've got to count the house." He pulled a pair of opera glasses from his pocket and began scrutinizing the crowd below. Frank sat down. His injured ear was throbbing, and he shifted uncomfortably in his seat.

After about ten minutes Orcrist put the glasses away and turned to Frank. "I'll be back soon," he said. "I've got to give your name to the registrar and pay your first month's dues. Don't leave the box." He waved and ducked out.

Frank leaned on the balcony rail, looked out over the restless throng, and soon saw Orcrist's dark, curly hair and drab cape appear from a side door. He watched him make his way to the speaker's stand and huddle for a moment with one of the men there. Frank's attention was distracted then by a fight that broke out in the middle of the hall, and when he glanced back at the speaker's stand Orcrist was gone. He was still trying to sight him when Orcrist's voice spoke softly behind him.

"Don't look so eager, Frank. Don't be conspicuous." The older man pulled a couple of chairs close to the rail. "Sit down and relax," he said. "This may take a while."

Frank had been expecting great things of this secret, underground meeting of thieves, but soon found himself bored. The speaker, a pudgy man named Hodges, spent the first few minutes exchanging casual jokes with members of the audience. Frank understood none of the references, though Orcrist frequently chuckled beside him. Hodges addressed everyone by their first names, and Frank felt more excluded than he had at any time in the past three days. He felt a little more at home when Hodges read the list of newly-bonded apprentices and he heard "Rovzar, Frank" read out as loudly as any of them.

What would Dad say, Frank wondered briefly, if he knew I was making a living as an art forger? He'd understand. As he once told me, while squinting against the sunlight of a cold morning, "Frankie, if it was easy, they'd have got somebody else to do it."

The meeting dragged on interminably, and just when Frank was convinced that he must fall asleep, a new figure appeared on the speaker's platform. It was a burly old man with a close-cropped white beard, and Frank saw the other officials who were standing about bow as the old man nodded to them.

"Who's that?" Frank asked.

"I thought you were asleep," Orcrist said. "That bearded guy? That's Blanchard. He's the king of the

Subterranean Companions. I expected to see him here. He must have heard about the palace rebellion—it's only something big that brings him to one of these meetings."

Blanchard now rapped the speaker's table with a fist. The crowd quieted much more quickly than it had for Hodges.

"My friends and colleagues," he began in a strong, booming voice. "I'm sure many of you have noticed evidences of a concealed crisis in the Ducal Palace." There was a pause while the more literate thieves explained the sentence to their slower-witted fellows. "Well, I am now able to tell you what's going on. Prince Costa has formed an alliance with the Transport Company and, day before yesterday, overthrown and killed Duke Topo." There were scattered cheers and outraged shouts. "We now have a new duke, gentlemen. It is too early to estimate the effects this change will have upon us and our operations, but I will say this: proceed with caution. The Transport spacers are no longer just drunken marks whose pockets you can pick and whose girls you can abuse. They are now our rulers. They will almost certainly function as police. Therefore I abjure you"—again there was a flurry of interpretation for the less bright thieves—"step carefully; don't cause unnecessary trouble; and keep your eyes open." The old man glared out at the cathedral-like hall. "I hope you ignorant bastards are paying attention. Maybe some of you remember Duke Ovidi, and how he hung a thief's head on every merlon of the Ducal Palace. Those days, friends, may very well be upon us once more."

On the way home from the meeting Frank's ear began to bleed again, and he passed out on the Sheol

Boulevard sidewalk. Orcrist carried him back to the apartment, changed his bandage and put him to bed.

FRANK tossed a paintbrush into a cup of turpentine and ran his hands through his unruly hair. It's going well, he thought. He'd been trying to get this painting in line for three days and had finally mastered Bate's style. He raised his head and stared at his still-wet painting, then turned and studied the original, hung next to it. I'll have this canvas finished this afternoon, Frank thought, which leaves the problem of darkening it and cracking it so that it looks as old as the original. But that was purely a technical detail, and he didn't anticipate any trouble with it.

The front door swung open and Orcrist strode in. He took off his black leather gloves and tossed them onto a chair.

"By God, Frank," he said, studying the forgery, "you have got the soul of Chandler Bate on canvas better than he did himself."

"Thanks," Frank said, wiping off a brush. "I've got to admit I'm pleased with it myself."

"It was the philosopher Aurelius," said Orcrist, sinking into his habitual easy chair, "who observed that 'the universe is change.' If he'd thought of it, he'd probably have added 'and an art forger's duties vary with the season.' "

"Ah. Are my duties about to vary?"

"As a matter of fact, they are." Orcrist poured two glasses of sherry and handed one to Frank. "For three weeks now you've been working away here, and you've copied four paintings and eleven drawings that I've brought you. Where do you suppose those art works have come from?"

"Stolen from museums and private collections," answered Frank promptly.

"Exactly. And whom do you suppose I had do the stealing?"

"I don't know."

"I'll tell you. A cousin of mine named Bob Dill. And two nights ago he was stabbed to death by a zealous pair of guards at the Amory Gallery. They chased him all over the building, hacking at him, and finally brought him down in the Pre-Raphaelite room."

Frank was unable to guess the appropriate response to this story, so he said nothing.

"What with one thing and another," Orcrist continued, "I find it impractical to hire another thief. The fine art market is suffering these days; Costa's damned taxes have taken up a good deal of the money that should rightfully go to people like you and me. The market isn't dead, you understand, just a trifle unsteady."

"So how will you get your paintings now?" Frank asked with a little trepidation.

"You and I will pinch them ourselves," Orcrist announced with a smile and a wave of his glass.

Frank had a quick vision of himself bleeding out the last of his lifeblood on the floor of the Pre-Raphaelite room. "Make Pons do it," he suggested.

"Now Frank, I know you don't mean that. I knew when I first saw you that you had an adventurer's heart. 'The lad's got an adventurer's heart,' I said to myself." Frank looked closely at Orcrist, unable to tell whether or not he was being kidded. "Besides," Orcrist went on, "I once gave Pons a chance to . . . prove himself under fire, and he absolutely failed to measure up. He's a fine doorman and butler, but he does *not* have an adventurer's heart."

"Oh," said Frank, wondering how adventurous his own heart really was.

"At any rate, Frank, we'll begin tonight. Since it's

your first crack at this sort of thing, I plan to start
with the Hauteur Museum. It's an easy place.''

''I'm glad of that.''

''Relax, you'll enjoy it. Now go get something to
eat. We'll leave at ten.''

As Frank crossed to the door, he heard a soft creak
behind it, and when he stepped into the hall he saw
the door of Pons's room being eased quietly shut.

THE Hauteur Museum had once been Munson's pride,
but with the building of several new theaters in the
Ishmael Village district to the north, the Hauteur
found itself no longer the heart of metropolitan cul-
ture. It was still well-thought-of when anyone did
think of it, and it could still boast some influential
paintings and sculptures, but its heyday had passed.

At eleven o'clock Frank and Orcrist entered its
cellar, having wormed their way up a laundry chute
that had once, when the Hauteur had been a hotel
two centuries before, emptied into a now-abandoned
sub-basement. Orcrist had carefully lifted off the ma-
hogany panel that hid the forgotten laundry chute.
''We want to replace it when we're done, you see,''
he told Frank in a whisper, ''in case we ever want to
come back again.''

They stole silently up the carpeted cellar stairs.
Their way was lit by moonlight filtering through
street-level grates set high in the walls, and Frank
realized with a pang of homesickness how long it had
been since he had seen real moonlight. I hope the
museum has windows, he thought.

The door at the top of the stairs was unlocked,
which Frank thought was careless of the owners. The
two adventurers swung it open as quietly as they
could. Orcrist motioned Frank to wait while he padded off into the darkness of the museum. Frank

waited nervously, only now beginning to realize just how much trouble this night's enterprise could lead to. Holy saints, he thought with a chill of real fear, if I'm caught they'll send me back to Barclay! I've still got that tattoo on my chest.

After a few uneasy minutes he heard a thump, then a multiple thud like a bag of logs thrown on a floor. God help us, he thought. What was that?

"Frank!" Orcrist's whisper cut the thick silence. "It's all clear! Carefully, now, go down the aisle on your left!"

When Frank did as he was told, he found himself in the main room. Paintings hung on every side, and he saw with delight a window opening on a quiet street and a deep, starry sky.

"Get away from the window, for God's sake," whispered Orcrist. Frank turned back to the room to see the older man standing over an unconscious uniformed body. "Come on," he hissed to Frank. "There are two paintings over here we ought to get."

Working in silence, Frank helped Orcrist unframe and roll two mediocre Havreville canvases. Orcrist thrust them inside his coat. "See anything else worth carrying?" he asked.

Frank was beginning to relax, and he strolled up and down the dim aisles, peering at paintings and statues with a critical eye. Not bad, most of it, he thought, but none of it seems worth the trouble to forge. I'm not even very impressed with those Havrevilles. As he turned to rejoin Orcrist he noticed, with a thrill of recognition, a small portrait hung between two gross seascapes. He stared intently at it, remembering the hot July day on which it had been painted. His father had been very fond of the model, and had frequently sent young Frank out for coffee or paint or simply ''fresh air.''

''Anything?'' Orcrist inquired impatiently.

''No,'' whispered Frank in reply. ''Let's clear out.''

Chapter 6

The Schilling Gallery, on which they made an assault four days later, was "not such an easy peach to pluck," as Orcrist was subsequently to observe to Frank. They failed to locate the drain that Orcrist swore would lead them directly into the gallery's office, and they had to bash a hole in the tile floor from beneath with an old wooden piling they found in the sewer. The noise was horribly loud, and they weren't in the gallery five minutes before armed guards were pounding at the doors. Orcrist refused to flee, though, determined to make off with a genuine Monet, which the Schilling had on loan from another planet.

"Let's get the hell *out* of here!" pleaded Frank, who saw the doors shaking as they were battered by boots and sword hilts on the other side. "One of them may have gone to get a key! We don't have thirty seconds!"

"Wait, I found it!" called Orcrist. He carefully

took the canvas out of its frame and rolled it. He was
sliding it into his pocket when the east door gave way
with a rending crack of splintering wood. Four yelling, sword-waving guards raced toward the two thieves.

Frank leaped sideways, grabbed a life-size bronze
statue of a man by the shoulder, and with a wrenching
effort pulled it over. It broke on the tiles directly in
front of the charging guards, and one of them pitched
headlong over the hollow trunk which was ringing
like a great bell from the impact of its fall. Frank
snatched up a cracked bronze arm and swung it at
another guard's head—it hit him hard over the eye
and he fell without a word.

"Come on, Frank!" called Orcrist, standing over
the jagged hole through which they'd entered. Frank
impulsively picked up one of the statue's ears, which
had broken off; then he ran toward Orcrist. The other
two guards were also running toward Orcrist from
the other side of the room, their rapiers held straight
out in front of them. Orcrist's hand darted under his
cape, and then the front of the cape exploded outward in a spray of fire, and the two guards were
slammed away from him as if they'd been hit by a
truck. They lay where they fell, their faces splashed
with blood and their uniforms torn up across the
front. The harsh smell of gunpowder rasped in Frank's
nose as he leaped down through the hole after Orcrist.

Twenty minutes later, as they caught their breath
in Orcrist's sitting room after a furtive race through a
dozen narrow, low-ceilinged understreet alleys, Frank
showed Orcrist the bronze ear he'd stolen.

"And what do you mean to do with that?" asked
Orcrist, painfully flexing his right hand.

"I'm going to run a string through it, and wear it
where my right ear used to be. Like an eye patch,
you know."

"An ear patch."

"Exactly," agreed Frank. "How's the Monet?"

Orcrist gingerly pulled the canvas out of his jacket and unrolled it. "No harm done," he said, examining it. "Monet is a durable painter."

"I guess so. What the hell was that weapon?" Frank asked in an awed tone.

"That impressed you, did it? That was a two-barrelled twelve gauge shotgun, barrels sawed down to six inches, and equipped with a pistol grip. I think I broke my hand shooting it. Ruined my cape for sure. We're lucky I didn't put the canvas in the line of fire."

Frank sighed wearily. "Mr. Orcrist, in honor of our coup tonight, do you suppose a bit of scotch would be out of order?"

"Not at all, Frank, help yourself." Frank opened the liquor cabinet. Orcrist sat silently, massaging the wrist and fingers of his right hand.

"Oh, by the way, Mr. Orcrist. . . ."

"Yes?"

"What becomes of the paintings once they're duplicated here? Do you sell both the original and the copy to collectors?"

"Uh . . . no. If I steal one painting and sell two versions of it, the word would eventually get around. I only sell the forgeries."

Frank waited vainly for Orcrist to go on. "Well," he said finally, "what do you do with the originals?"

Orcrist looked up. "I keep them. I'm a collector myself, you see."

DURING the following week Frank worked on the forgery of the Monet. It was difficult for him to assume the impressionist style, and he tore up two attempts with a palette knife. As the second imperfect copy was being hacked into ragged strips, Orcrist, sitting in his easy chair, looked up from his book.

"Not making a lot of headway?" he asked.

"No," said Frank, trying to keep a rein on his temper. What a cheap waste of good canvas, he thought. Dad never would have behaved this childishly. Where's my discipline?

"What you need, Frank, is a bit of recreation. Go spend some of your wages. You know the safe areas of Understreet Munson—go have some beer at Huselor's, it's a good place."

"Yeah, maybe I'll do that. Say, what's the date?"

"The tenth. Of May. Why?"

"The Doublon Festival is going on in Munson! On the surface, I mean. I haven't missed it in the last six years! Why don't I take my wages and spend the evening there?"

Orcrist frowned doubtfully. "That wouldn't be a good idea," he said. "You can't really afford to be seen topside yet. You're wanted by the police, you know. Stay underground."

"It'll be all right," Frank insisted. "I'll go when it's dark; and everyone wears masks anyway. You've shown me a couple of safe routes to the surface streets, and I've been to the Doublon Festival a dozen times, so I won't get lost. I won't do anything foolish."

"I'll send a couple of bodyguards with you, anyway."

"No, I'd rather be on my own."

Orcrist considered it for a minute. "Well, it's a bad idea, but I won't stop you." He stood up and crossed to a desk against the wall. "Be back by one o'clock in the morning or I'll send some rough friends to bring you back. Here's ten malories. That ought to buy you a good time."

Frank gratefully took the money and turned to get dressed.

"Wait a minute," said Orcrist.

Frank turned around in the doorway. Orcrist was rummaging in another drawer. "Take this, too, in case of a *real* emergency," he said, holding a small silver pistol. "It only holds one bullet, but it's a forty-five. And don't lose it; the damned thing cost me quite a bit."

"I won't lose it," said Frank, taking the little gun. It was the first time he'd ever held a gun, and he felt ridiculously over-armed.

"The safety catch is that button above the trigger. Push it in and the gun will shoot. Leave it where it is for now. And for God's sake keep it in a secure pocket."

"I will," said Frank. "And thanks. Don't worry, I'll be careful."

After Frank had left the room, Orcrist rang for Pons. "Pons," he said, "young Rovzar is determined to go to the Doublon Festival tonight. I could have forbidden it, of course, but I don't like to operate that way. So I want you to contact Bartlett and . . . oh, Fallworth, and tell them to follow him and keep an eye on him."

"Yes sir."

"No, dammit. Wait a minute." Orcrist scowled. "I guess he's able to take care of himself. Forget it, Pons."

"With pleasure, sir."

FRANK dressed in the subdued clothes Orcrist had given him, put on his newly-polished bronze ear, and then left the apartment, the gun and the ten malories each occupying a safe inner pocket. He cut across Sheol to a street that was really little more than a tunnel. After following it for three hundred feet, he turned suddenly to the right, into an alcove that could not be seen a yard away. It led into a much narrower, darker tunnel, and Frank proceeded slowly, his hand on his knife. He still didn't think of the gun as a practical weapon.

Water swirled around his heels, and he was glad when his groping right hand found the rungs of the ladder he'd been heading for. He climbed up it through a round brick shaft whose sides were slippery with moss and flowing water, and eventually came to the underside of a manhole cover. This he pushed up cautiously, peering about carefully before sliding it aside. He quickly climbed out of the shaft and pushed the manhole cover back into place with his foot.

He was now on the surface, breathing fresh night air for the first time in almost a month. The stars looked beautifully distant, and he felt almost uneasy to see no roof overhead. The manhole was several blocks away from Kudeau Street, where the Doublon Festival was held, but he could hear the shouts and music already.

I've been cooped up too long in that little sewer world, he realized. Let's see how much money I can spend in one night.

He followed the alley to Pantheon Boulevard and headed east toward Kudeau Street. Long before he reached it, he was surrounded by masked dancers, and the curbs were crowded with the crepe-decorated plywood stands of vendors. The music was a crashing, howling thing, yelping out of guitars, slide whistles, trumpets and kazoos, and crowds reeled drunkenly down the streets, swaying unevenly to the chaotic melody. The warm night air smelled of garlic and beer.

Frank bought a sequined cardboard mask and a cup

of cloudy, potent beer from the nearest booth. After putting on the mask and downing the beer at a gulp, he joined the dancing mob. He linked arms with a groaning rummy on his right and a startlingly fat woman on his left, following Pantheon's tide of revellers as they emptied slowly into the packed expanse of Kudeau Street. The moon was up now, shining full behind the ragged Munson skyline.

After an hour of dancing and drinking, Frank stumbled over a curb and crossed the sidewalk to lean against a pillar and catch his breath. He was somewhat drunk, but he could see a great difference in the Dublon Festival this year; in past years, when he had come with his father, it had been a festive, fairly formalized celebration of the spring.

This year it was something else. Screams that began as singing were degenerating into insane shrieks. The dancing had become a huge game of snap-the-whip, and people were being flung spinning from the end of the line with increasing force. People had stopped paying for the beer. Couples were making frantic love in doorways, under the vendors' booths, even in the street. And over all, from every direction, skirled the maddening noise that could no longer really be called music.

Time for a decision, Frank told himself. Go home now or stay and take whatever consequences are floating around unclaimed. I need another beer to decide, he compromised, and began elbowing his way toward a beer-seller's stand.

Before he reached it he sensed a change in the crowd. People paused, and were craning their necks, peering up and down the street.

"What is it?" Frank shouted to the man next to him.

"Costa!" the man answered. "The Duke!"

Frank looked around but could see nothing because
of the crowd. His drunkenness left him, and he felt a
cold emptiness in his stomach. *Costa!* he thought.
Here! He ducked into the nearest building, ran up the
stairs, and blundered his way out onto a second floor
balcony that overlooked the choked street.

From this vantage point he saw the procession
bulling its way through the mob of drunken, torch-
waving revellers; he saw the elegant litter being carried at shoulder height and the languid youth who
waved from within at the merrymakers. Even from a
distance of fifty feet he recognized the pale, con-
temptuous face of Costa, the parricide, the Duke who
had had Frank's father killed.

He can't see me in the shadow of the awning here,
Frank thought. Even if he could, I'm masked. He
drew his coat tighter about his chest to cover his
damning tattoo, and his fingers brushed the lump
under the fabric that covered the gun. Suddenly and
completely, he knew what he had to do. The shot
wouldn't be difficult at this range, and a forty-five
calibre bullet ought to do the job.

Trembling, he took the gun out of his pocket and
pushed off the safety catch. The procession had drawn
even with him in the street. Costa was as close now
as he would ever be. Stepping back, Frank raised the
gun. I *can't*, he thought. There must be twenty guards
down there. Some of them have guns, and I've only
got one bullet. I'd never get away through this crowd.
I *can't*.

He stood there, shaking, with the gun pointed at
Costa's face. The procession was slowly moving past.
In another few seconds he'll be out of my line of
sight, Frank thought.

There was a commotion in the crowd below, and a
man ran at the litter and jumped up onto its running

board. Frank saw a brief gleam of moonlight on a knife blade. Four quick gunshots broke the continuity of the crazy music, and the man with the knife stumbled to the ground. His weapon fell on the paving stones. He walked lurchingly back toward the crowd, and Frank could see the blood on his shirt. Two more shots cracked, and the man fell sideways onto the street.

Costa leaned out of the litter and waved to show that he was unhurt. The guards cheered, but the crowd almost booed him. An ugly tension was building; Costa and his attendants left quickly.

Frank replaced the gun in his pocket, feeling sick. He returned to Orcrist's underground apartment, stopping twice along the route to throw up.

THE next morning he gave Orcrist back his gun and told him about the abortive assassination attempt by the man with the knife.

"I heard about it," Orcrist said. "I knew the man slightly."

"It was a crazy thing to do," Frank declared.

"Yes, it was. Did you hear that Costa has abolished the Doublon Festival? He said it's a 'free-for-all crime fest,' to use his words. It won't even finish out the week, as it normally would."

"It was pretty wild last night. I've been to it a dozen times and it was never nearly as bad as it was last night."

"That's because times were prosperous under old Duke Topo. Times are very bad now and getting worse; that's why the festival was such a madhouse. People figured it was their last chance to enjoy themselves, and they'd do it or know the reason why."

"Times aren't *that* bad, are they?"

"I don't know, Frank. They seem to be. The

Transport is a bankrupt organization, but determined not to admit it. The interplanetary shipping lines are collapsing. The Transport seems to have decided to make Octavio its home planet, and so Costa, having sold out to them, is taxing the guts out of the people to support it. The end isn't in sight—and we haven't even hit bottom yet.''

Chapter 7

Two months later Orcrist once again had occasion to quote Aurelius to Frank.

"You see, Frank," he explained, "when a man proves himself capable, he is likely to be given more tasks. You began as simply an art forger, and then also took on the duties of a quality art procurer."

"Am I about to take on someone else's duties? Did you lose another cousin?" Frank's bronze ear gleamed in the lamplight.

"What a horrible thing to say, Frank. But yes, as a matter of fact, I was thinking of broadening your functions, giving you some experience in another field—now that my art collectors are so tax-strangled and the museums so heavily guarded and our night runs are becoming so few and far between."

"My new field being . . . ?"

"Well, I entertain quite a bit, you know. Pons handles the details quite well, but the kitchen is a chaos. Kitchen boys come and go like sailors in a brothel, and now my chief cook has walked out. So I thought that, in the free time between our night runs and your painting, you might help Pons out with the dinners, cooking and washing up, and all.''

Frank swallowed the indignant anger that Orcrist's suggestion raised in him. *Take it easy*, he thought. Orcrist's employment is all that stands between you and the lean life of a fugitive. He's fed you and taken care of you, and it isn't his fault that the new government has made affluence an archaic word. Orcrist works as hard as you do (harder, probably), and risks his neck as well as your own on the night raids.

"What do you say?" asked Orcrist, and Frank suddenly realized that the older man was embarrassed to be making the request.

"It sounds okay to me," Frank said. "I guess a little kitchen experience is a valuable thing to have."

"Of course it is," Orcrist agreed heartily. "I propose we celebrate it with a couple of glasses of this excellent Tamarisk brandy."

After downing his brandy Frank went to the kitchen to get acquainted with the layout. He found Pons sitting on a stool, nibbling a chunk of Jack cheese. The tall, skinny servant regarded Frank skeptically.

"Don't tell me you took it," he said.

"Matter of fact, I did," answered Frank. "What is it I do?"

Pons stood up and ran his fingers through his graying hair. "Well now, you'll find that kitchen work isn't as easy as painting." He peered at Frank, who said nothing. "But at least it's *honest* work." Frank smiled coldly.

Encouraged by Frank's silence, Pons grinned and took another bite of cheese. "Yessir," he said. "Liquor and books is all very well, but you don't get time for that sort of trash in here. You know what I say?''

''What do you say?''

''I say, if you've got time enough to lean, you've got time enough to clean. Now we don't have to get started on dinner for another two hours yet, so why don't you get a rag and a bucket of hot water and clean off the oven hood? And then after that you can clean out these drains. What?''

''I didn't say anything,'' said Frank.

''Well, see that you don't. I don't like noisy help.'' Pons took his cheese and left the room, on his lips the smile of the man who has had the last word.

Now *what*, thought Frank, have I done to provoke all that? He looked helplessly around himself at the kitchen. A big, gleaming oven stood in the center of the room. Around the walls were sinks and refrigerators and freezers. Years of airborne grease had darkened the yellow walls near the ceiling.

With a fatalistic sigh he began looking for a mop, a rag and a bucket.

WHEN Pons returned at four, he criticized Frank's cleaning and asked him if his father and he had been accustomed to living in a pigpen.

''No,'' said Frank evenly. I will deal with this Pons fellow, he told himself, when the opportunity arises.

''Well, that's what anyone would think, to see the lazy-man job you did on these sinks.'' He looked around the room with a dissatisfied air. ''It's high time we got started on dinner. And let me tell you, sonny, the best way to get on Sam's bad side is to serve him bad food.''

Spare me your pompous master-chef act, thought

Frank. And I'd like to see you call him Sam to his face.

"He's having eight guests to dinner tonight, and I'm serving them chicken curry. Chop a pound apiece of green onions and peanuts and put them in those silver bowls up there. Also, fill two more bowls with chutney and raisins. Then decant six bottles of the Rigby Chablis, which you'll find in the cooler yonder. Do you think you can handle all that?"

"Time will tell," said Frank with false gaiety, hoping it would annoy Pons, as he set out to find the onions and peanuts.

WHEN the guests had all arrived, the table was set and dinner was ready to be served, Pons strode into the kitchen and grabbed Frank's arm.

"I've got to keep an eye on things here," he said. "You serve the dinner."

"*Me*? I don't know anything about it! I can't serve the damned dinner!"

"Keep your voice down. Of course you can serve it. I'm giving you a chance to . . . prove yourself under fire, you might say. Here's the wine. Go!"

Frank swung through the kitchen doors into the dining room, carrying a silver tray on which were perched two decanters of Chablis and eight glasses, all clinking dangerously. He had to set the tray down carefully on the tablecloth before he dared raise his eyes to the assembled company.

The first eyes he met were Orcrist's, who looked both surprised and angry. The two white-haired men flanking him looked amused, and their two thin old women regarded Frank with discreet distaste. Bad business, Frank thought, as he pulled desperately at the crystal stopper on one of the decanters. On the other side of the table sat a slender man with slick, gleaming hair; he winked at Frank. Next to him was a good-looking young woman with deep brown eyes and slightly kinky brown hair; very close to her sat a healthy-looking young man who was clearly holding the girl's hand under the table.

Some guests, Frank thought. He'd got the stopper out, poured a half inch of wine into one glass and gravely passed it to Orcrist. This may not be correct, he thought, but at least it's formal.

Orcrist raised his eyebrows, but took the glass. He sipped it and nodded. Frank filled the glass, and then proceeded to fill all the glasses, moving clockwise around the table. When he had finished he set the decanter in the middle of the table, bowed, and fled into the kitchen.

"How'd it go?" asked Pons.

"Not bad. What's next?"

"Salad. In five minutes. Put the dressing on it in four and a half minutes."

As Frank strode out carrying the salad bowl five minutes later, he felt a premonition of disaster. Pons had thrown a handful of garbanzo beans on top of the salad at the last minute, and Frank, foreseeing them rolling all over the table, thought it an unwise move.

I'll serve the pretty girl first, he thought. He walked smiling to her place and holding the bowl in one hand, reached for the salad tongs with the other. Smooth, he told himself.

Pons had, earlier, set the bowl down in a puddle of salad oil, and now Frank's grip on the bowl slipped an inch. A garbanzo bean rolled off the mound of lettuce and plunked into the girl's wine. She squealed. Her escort turned a face of outrage on Frank, who tried to back away and perhaps get a new wine glass.

"Idiot!" barked the escort as he stood up, shoving his chair violently backward against Frank's leg. The greased salad bowl left Frank's hand, rolled over in the air, and landed on the brown-eyed girl's chest, from there sliding down into her lap. Covered with gleaming lettuce, carrots and garbanzo beans, the surprised girl looked like a tropical hillside.

"For God's *sake*, Frank!" boomed Orcrist after a stunned pause. "Go get Pons!"

Frank hurried into the kitchen. "You take over," he told Pons, and then went to his room, feeling monumentally inadequate.

AFTER the guests had left, Orcrist asked Frank to accompany him on a walk. Frank nodded and fetched a coat. They walked for two blocks along an empty stretch of Sheol before Orcrist spoke.

"Bad show, there, Frank."

"That's true, sir."

They walked on, past another block.

"I am not going to relieve you of your kitchen duties, though. Oh, I know it was an accident! That's not what I mean. I think you should continue to work in the kitchen, under Pons's direction, for the same reason I'd tell you to keep trying to ride a horse that had thrown you, or to keep practicing fencing after you'd taken a bad cut. Don't let these things defeat you, eh?"

"Right," agreed Frank without much enthusiasm.

"Good. Kathrin Figaro's boyfriend wanted to cut your throat, by the way. I told him he'd probably need a bit of help, and he stormed out. Next time, spill the salad on him."

Frank laughed weakly.

"A penny to see a dancing dog?" came a plaintive cry from the alleymouth they were passing. Orcrist stepped aside and handed the old woman some coins before he and Frank continued their walk.

"That was Beardo's mother," Orcrist remarked. "They don't get along real well."

Frank didn't say anything.

THE next time he saw Kathrin Figaro he was relaxing in Orcrist's sitting room, having finished his forgery of the difficult Monet canvas. He was dressed in an old pair of jeans and a T-shirt, over which he had thrown the white silk smoking jacket Beardo had given him.

The front door opened just as Frank was pouring himself a well deserved (he told himself) glass of scotch. Assuming that it was Orcrist, he spoke casually over his shoulder. "I figured you wouldn't mind my taking a glass, sir," he said, and turned around to see Orcrist standing in the doorway with Miss Figaro on his arm.

"You've grown lax in your treatment of kitchen boys, Sam," said Miss Figaro sharply. She stepped forward and slapped the glass out of Frank's hand. It bounced on the carpet, splashing scotch on the bookshelves.

"I hate this sort of thing," declared Orcrist. "Kathrin, he *isn't* a kitchen boy. He's an apprenticed thief, and a junior partner of mine. Frank, pour yourself another glass. Pour me one too. Will you join us, Kathrin?"

"No," she said icily. "Why is he dressed like a hobo mandarin? And why do you have him serve dinner if he's a junior partner?" Plainly, she thought Orcrist was having a joke at her expense.

"I was doing that because we felt I'd be better off for some kitchen experience," explained Frank, who was beginning to enjoy this. "And I'm dressed in my painting clothes. This is a smoking jacket."

"He paints as well, does he?"

"Yes," Orcrist answered. "It's a hobby of his. Still lifes, puppies, sad children with big eyes—you know."

Kathrin looked close to tears. "Sam, if you and this horrible boy are making fun of me, I'll. . . ."

"We're not, I swear," said Orcrist placatingly as he put his arm around her shoulders. "Frank, draw something, show her we're not kidding."

"All right." There was a salt shaker on the coffee table, a relic of a bout of tequila drinking the night before, and Frank shook salt onto the dark tabletop until it had a uniformly frosted look. Then, with his left forefinger, he drew a quick picture of Kathrin. It caught a likeness, and even conveyed some of her apparently habitual irritability.

"There, you see?" said Orcrist. "I wasn't kidding."

"You aren't a kitchen boy?"

"Not basically, no," Frank answered.

"Oh. Well then, I'm sorry I spilled your drink. No, I'm not! You ruined my dress."

"Let's forget all of it," said Orcrist, "and be friends."

"Okay," said Frank agreeably.

"All right." Kathrin still seemed sulky.

The afternoon progressed civilly, and once, when Orcrist left the room, Kathrin turned to Frank with a hesitant smile.

"Could you . . . teach me how to draw, sometime?"

She looks much younger when she smiles, he thought. I'll bet she's about my age.

"Sure," he said.

RAIN was somehow falling down the sunlight shaft onto Orcrist's breakfast table. Frank sat watching it drip onto the remains of his scrambled eggs; he was puffing at a pipe and wondering how the devil pipe smokers kept the things lit. Across the table George Tyler was slumped dejectedly in a chair, his blond hair sticking out at odd angles from his head.

Orcrist walked in, carrying a plate of fried eggs and bacon and potatoes. "What's this?" he asked, nodding at the growing puddle of rain water.

"It's raining on the surface," said Frank. "I suppose we ought to put a pan under it." He resumed puffing on the pipe.

"Oh, your plate will do for now," Orcrist said. "What are you trying to smoke?"

Frank waved at a pack of tobacco lying on the table. Orcrist picked it up and stared at it. " 'Cherry Brandy Flavored.' Frank, you can't smoke *that*." He tossed it down. "Let me get you some *real* tobacco."

"And what's *real* tobacco?" asked Tyler irritably. It had been he who'd recommended the Cherry Brandy blend to Frank.

"Something with latakia in it," Orcrist said. "This fruit syrup stuff is no good for smoking; it's only fit for impressing ignorant girls."

Tyler shrugged, as if to say that that was reason enough to smoke it right there.

"Anyway, I have better things to talk about than bad tobacco," Orcrist went on. "Tomorrow night I'm giving a dinner for ten of the High Lords of the Subterranean Companions. I'm hiring three guys to help out in the kitchen; you and Pons will be in charge, Frank. We're going to have Giant Tacos, Beans Jaimé, and dark beer—I've got Pons out buying supplies now. I think you ought to be the beer steward, Frank; you simply stand by with a pitcher of it and refill any glasses that become less than half full."

"Doesn't sound bad," Frank said. "Will anyone I know be there?"

"No, she won't," said Orcrist.

THE next afternoon Frank strolled into the kitchen, where Pons and the three new cooks were already at work. One of the new men was chopping bell peppers on a wooden board; another was stirring a pot of hot sauce; and the third was grating block after block of cheese. On a stool to one side sat Pons, criticizing their work and telling them what needed doing afterward.

"It's about time you got here," Pons said. "Keep an eye on these dopes for a while." He got up and strode out, shaking his head contemptuously.

"Oh, man," said one of the cooks. "Who *was* that guy?"

"His name's Pons," said Frank. "I don't like him either. Do you guys know how to do all this? Because I sure can't tell you."

"Oh, hell yes," said another. "We work in a restaurant together. We've been making this stuff since we were kids. And then old Bon-Bon comes in here and wants to tell me how to cut bell peppers."

"Well, cut them any way you want," said Frank.

The big oven was turned on, and the room heated up pretty quickly, especially when one of the cooks began frying the ground beef in two huge pans. Frank was only doing peripheral jobs, chopping onions and fetching tomatoes, but he soon found himself sweating like a long-distance runner.

"Listen," he said, "I'm ready for a beer. Who'll join me?"

They all assented, and Frank opened four bottles of Orcrist's favorite light beer. He passed these around, and then was amazed at how much more smoothly the kitchen ran when the cooks had bottles of beer beside them. There's some principle at work there, he thought.

The door was kicked open and Pons entered.

"You're letting them *drink?*" he gasped. He snatched all the bottles, which were empty now anyway, and flung them into a trash can. "Sam will hear about this," he snarled at Frank. "You'll be out of a job."

"I don't think so," Frank said.

"Clear out, Bon-Bon," said one of the cooks.

"You've gone too far," Pons whispered. "You can't undermine me. Tomorrow you'll be out on the *street*."

"Time will tell," smiled Frank.

"The guests are here," said Pons in a strangled voice. "Take out fifteen glasses and two pitchers of beer. Now!"

Frank did so, and managed without mishap to present each guest with a glass of the dark beer. There were ten, all older men, and they were dressed in fine clothes and wore decorated swords. When Frank had filled their glasses he stepped back from the table, but Orcrist beckoned him forward.

"Gentlemen," Orcrist said, "I'd like you to meet Francisco de Goya Rovzar, my junior partner." Orcrist introduced Frank to each lord in turn. Frank bowed respectfully to each, and then resumed his stewardship. The lords and Orcrist chatted and laughed among themselves, and Frank listened in from time to time, but found their talk either boring or incomprehensible.

Eventually Pons appeared, pushing a cart on which were set ten plates, each with a huge taco resting on it like a giant, lettuce-choked clam. The assembled lords exclaimed delightedly at the spectacle. Pons served them, and the guests began hesitantly prodding their tacos with forks. Frank was kept busy seeing that the glasses were filled and frequently had to dash to the kitchen for a fresh pitcher.

"Damn fine dinner, Sam," said Lord Tolley Christensen as he threw down his fork for the last time. The other lords all nodded agreement. "And I hope such dinners never become a thing of the past." Again they all nodded.

"Do you know, Tolley," spoke up Lord Rutledge, "I was walking alone the other day or night and an armed policeman, in the Transport uniform, tried to *arrest* me?"

"Times are worse than I thought," said Orcrist. "What did you do?"

"Oh, he drew his sword on me, so I killed him."

"How?" asked Tolley. "As one craftsman to another."

"He took my blade on the outside of his, in the high line, so I did a non-resisting parry and then just spiralled in over his bell guard, then under it, and nailed him."

"He must not have been real sharp," put in Orcrist. "I'd never have given you time to do all that."

"Well, I *am* fairly fast," Rutledge said. "Besides, that's the only move you can make if the other guy takes your blade that way."

"Well," spoke Frank, "you *could* parry and riposte in prime."

"What?" growled Rutledge, shifting around in his chair.

"I said you could have parried him in prime. One, you know."

"What the hell do you mean?"

Frank was beginning to suspect that he shouldn't have spoken. "Never mind, sir," he said. "I'm sorry I interrupted."

"Wait a minute," said Orcrist. "Here, Frank, use

my sword. Rutledge, will you let me borrow yours for a moment? Thank you. Now, Frank, *slowly*, show me what you mean.''

Frank put the pitcher of beer down on a side table, took the sword in his left hand, and crouched into the on guard position. ''All right,'' he said. ''Take my blade in sixte—come in over my sword arm.''

Orcrist extended his blade as he was told. When the point was within a foot of Frank's chest, Frank suddenly inverted his sword by flipping his elbow up and deflected Orcrist's blade to the side; then he riposted, thrusting at Orcrist's chest with his arm twisted around so that his thumb and fingers were uppermost.

''That's parrying in prime,'' he said, holding the position with his point an inch or two away from Orcrist's chest. ''It's a bit awkward, but if you use it at the right moment it's unanswerable.''

''The boy's making fun of us,'' growled Rutledge.

''Maybe not,'' said Orcrist. ''Let's try a few thrusts, Frank. Gently.''

For the first minute Frank let Orcrist do all the work, and simply parried every thrust without even stepping back. Orcrist's thrusts became faster and stronger, but Frank was able to hold him off effortlessly. He can't really be trying, Frank thought. These attacks are fairly quick, but there's almost no strategy.

''Shall I begin replying?'' asked Frank.

''Any time you like,'' panted Orcrist.

Frank parried the next attack and feinted in quarte, then riposted in sixte to Orcrist's chest, poking him lightly with the point. He then tapped Orcrist's elbow twice in a row, and then did a faultless bind-eight culminating in a full-extension lunge. He held the position for a moment; his rear leg straight out behind him, lead leg bent in a ninety-degree angle, weapon arm straight and his sword point pressing a button on Orcrist's coat. Then he relaxed back into the on guard posture. It felt good to get back into the disciplines of fencing—it reminded him of the old days with Tom in the Strand Fencing Academy.

"There is . . . no end to your talents, Frank," Orcrist panted. "Where did you study? Who taught you all this?"

"Jacob Strand, in a fencing school about twenty miles north and ten miles west."

"Hmm." Orcrist sat down and finished his beer. "Do you remember the words of our old friend Aurelius, Frank?"

"Yes, I do. 'The universe is change.' Might he have added 'and talented lads are soon promoted out of the kitchen'?"

"Consider it added," said Orcrist.

BOOK TWO: The Swordsman

Chapter 1

Frank delivered a final poke to the man-shaped
rubber pad that was nailed to the wall—got him right
in the throat!—and put down his sword. He unbut-
toned his fencing jacket and sat down in a nearby
canvas chair. Now where the hell is old Rutledge?
Frank glanced at the clock on the wall. He's ten
minutes late.

Frank stood up, crossed to the open window, and
leaned on the sill. He watched the littered tide of the
Leethee flow past, its blackness highlighted by dancing glints of light cast by the lamps that hung from
the tunnel roof. The river was wide through here, and
he sometimes saw festive barges and solitary canoes
wend their way up or downstream.

The Rovzar Fencing School had been open for
almost six weeks. The location was good (Orcrist had
helped him find a good river-view building to rent in
a respectable neighborhood), and he already had
enough students to pay the rent and keep him busy.

Without exception, his students were ranking members of the Subterranean Companions; Orcrist pointed out that there was no reason to teach fencing secrets to strangers.

A chittering screech sounded in the adjoining room, and Frank turned around with a smile as Rutledge entered, carrying his pet monkey on his shoulder.

"Down, Bones!" Rutledge commanded. Bones, a wild-eyed spider monkey, leaped from the lord's shoulder onto a chair and began gnawing the fabric.

"Damn all monkeys," growled Rutledge. He shrugged off his velvet coat and took a fencing jacket out of a closet. "You must have washed these, Rovzar! This one seems to have shrunk."

"It's possible," Frank said. It's not the jacket's fault, he thought. It's beer and pork pie that have tightened the fit. "Have you been practicing your on guard?"

"Yes, yes. It's invincible." Rutledge flipped a wire-mesh fencing mask over his face and selected one of the practice épées hanging on a wall rack. He flexed the blade a few times and then crouched, the blade held forward and ready. "How's that?" he asked.

Frank put on a mask and picked up his own épée.

"Not bad," he said, critically examining Rutledge's posture. "Let's see if you can maintain it."

He saluted, and they began to bout, starting slow and relaxed. Each point hovered around the other man's bell guard, never getting a clear shot at a wrist or forearm. After a minute, Frank began to let his elbows show beneath, apparently unguarded. He saw Rutledge tense with preparation, and then the lord's blade flashed out at Frank's elbow. Just as he saw him extend, though, Frank went up on his toes and straightened his sword arm, catching Rutledge in the biceps with the sword's covered tip. Rutledge's sword wavered in empty air.

"That's a favorite trick of mine," Frank explained. "Lure him below with your elbow and then go in over the top when he goes for it. You've got to be quick, though, or you'll have a hole in your arm and an opponent who thinks you're an idiot."

"Give me a gun anytime," Rutledge said. "When I was a boy we had guns, you know. Kill a man from across a courtyard! None of this damned personal contact."

"Yes," Frank said, "but a gun doesn't take much skill. Any stable boy could kill you with a gun. But how many people can kill you with a sword?"

"Not many! Especially now that I'm taking your lessons. Your damnably expensive lessons." Frank shrugged. "How do I compare with your other students, Rovzar? I know Orcrist and a few others are studying your methods. Has Tolley come in?"

"No, Lord Christensen doesn't think he needs any help. He told Orcrist that the day he goes to a painter for fencing lessons will be the day he sends Costa his two virgin daughters. Not real soon, in other words. Anyhow, speaking honestly, I'd say you're my most rapidly improving student."

"No kidding?" replied Rutledge in a pleased tone of voice. "In that case have another try at teaching me that eye shot."

The next half hour was spent in showing the elderly lord a particularly vicious bind in sixte that, properly executed, landed one's point forcefully in the opponent's eye. Rutledge was beginning to catch on, and after Frank had three times taken a blow to his mask he called a recess.

"I pity any sewer vagabonds who try to rob you," Frank said. He opened a cabinet and took a bottle of cheap *vino blanco* out of an ice bucket. "Will you join me in some wine, my lord?"

"Good God, yes. Swordplay is dry work."

Rutledge took a glass of wine and gulped half of it right off. Bones climbed up to his belt buckle and made gross smacking sounds, so Rutledge handed the monkey the glass, and the hairy creature drank the rest of it with relish.

"Can monkeys get drunk?" asked Rutledge.

"I suppose so. Want me to give him a glass?"

"Why don't you."

Frank poured a third, slightly bigger glass, and handed it to Bones. The monkey took it to a corner to drink, and Frank poured another glass to replace Rutledge's slobbery one.

"There is a nice feint you can use if your man bends his arm as he retreats," said Frank, crossing to the windowsill and sitting down on it. "Done right, it puts your point into his kneecap. I'll have to show it to you next."

"Why do so few of your moves hit the body, Rovzar?" asked Rutledge. "Seems to me you're just wasting time hitting your opponent in the arm and the knee."

"If your opponent knows anything about swords, you generally can't *get* to the body," Frank told him. "Before your point hits his stomach or chest, his point is buried in your forearm. A full-extension lunge is a beautiful thing to do when you're practicing in a fencing school, but I'd certainly never do one in an alley against an opponent with an untipped weapon."

Frank was suddenly aware of breathing sounds echoing softly behind him, from the river. He leaped off of the sill and turned around, pushing his sweaty hair out of his eyes. Peripherally, he saw Rutledge come up beside him and stare wordlessly out.

The river was jammed. Boats, rafts and logs covered its surface, and every floating thing carried silent, staring passengers. Children huddled in blankets in the bows of rowboats, while haggard old men worked the oars; string-tied bundles and frying pans and guitars were roped in piles on rafts that old women paddled along with boards; sunken-eyed men floated past with their arms around logs, their bodies immersed in water up to their chests. None of these drifters spoke, even to each other.

"What in God's name?" began Rutledge. Bones climbed unsteadily up his master's leg and perched beside him on the windowsill.

"Who are you?" called Frank to the people on the nearest raft. "Where are you all going?"

A man stood up on the raft. He looked about forty, with brown hair beginning to go gray at the temples; he wore overalls with no shirt under them. "We're farmers," he said, "from the Goriot Valley." The echoes of his own voice seemed to upset him, and he sat down again.

"Where are you going?" repeated Frank.

"To the Deptford Sea," answered a woman from a heavily-loaded rowboat. "We can't go overland because we don't have travel permits."

"Give us the monkey," called a boy perched on a log. "We don't have food. Give us the monkey, at least."

"Yes, the monkey, give it to us," came a shout from farther out in the river. In a moment the waterborne fugitives were chorusing madly: "The monkey!" "God save you for your gift of the monkey!" "My boy here hasn't eaten! Throw the monkey to me!"

Frank looked down at Bones, who squatted drunkenly on the stone coping of the window, blinking his
eyes at the clamoring floaters. The monkey's stomach
was jerking up and down like an adam's apple, and
as Frank watched, the beast leaned forward and nois-
ily vomited *vino blanco* into the water.

"Give us the damned monkey! We'll have it! You
can't keep it from us!" moaned and wailed the refugees. Frank leaned out and pulled the heavy shutters
closed. He latched them, and then slid a bolt through
the iron staples.

"Let's close up shop," he said to Rutledge. "You
were my last pupil of the day anyway."

They hung up the swords and jackets, blew out the
lamps, and locked the front door behind them. The
Rovzar Fencing School was in a fashionable understreet
neighborhood, so they talked freely and left their
swords in the scabbards as they walked. Spicy cooking smells wafted out of restaurant doors, and Frank
was beginning to get hungry.

"Have you paid off your bond to Orcrist yet?"
Rutledge asked.

"No," Frank answered, "but with the money I'm
making from the fencing classes, I should have it
paid off in a month or so."

"You'll be getting digs of your own then, I expect."

"Yes. I've been looking at apartments here in the
Congreve district, and I think I could afford to live
near the school, which would be handy."

They rounded a corner and found themselves facing four uniformed Transport policemen, each armed
with a standard-issue rapier. Their faces showed tan
in the lamplight, proof that they were new to understreet work.

"Good evening, gentlemen," grinned one of the

Transports. "May I see your identification and employment cards?"

"Since when have they been necessary for understreet citizens?" queried Rutledge with icy politeness.

"Since Duke Costa signed a law saying so, weasel! Now trot 'em out or come along with us to the station." Each policeman's hand was on his sword hilt.

Rutledge drew his sword with a salty curse. Frank and the four Transports followed suit simultaneously. One of the Transports lunged at Rutledge, who parried and jabbed the man in the wrist. Bones, terrified, leaped from the lord's shoulder to the ground.

"Nicely done!" called Frank to Rutledge as two of the Transports centered on him. He feinted ferociously at one, and the man retreated a full two steps. The other man aimed a beat at Frank's blade, but Frank dropped his point to elude it and then gored the man deeply in the shoulder. The clanging and rasp of the swords rang up and down the street. Frank stole another glance at Rutledge and saw the lord thrusting furiously at one of his opponents.

"Watch your weapon arm!" Frank shouted. "Hide behind your bell guard! Don't be impatient!" Frank held his two men off by whirling his point in a continuous horizontal figure eight. It was dangerous, but it gained him a breathing space. After a few seconds the shoulder-wounded Transport got angry and ran at Frank in an ill-considered fleche attack; Frank stepped away from the blade and drove his point through the man's neck. The other policeman was close behind, so Frank hopped backward as he pulled his sword free. Bright red blood jetted as the stricken Transport sank to his knees on the street.

"How goes it, my lord?" Frank called as he crossed swords with his remaining opponent.

"I poked one of them in the belly," gasped Rutledge. "Be careful . . . he's crawling around in the middle of the street. Don't let him get you . . . from below."

Frank glimpsed the man, who was on his hands and knees on the pavement, and kept clear of him. Frank tried two feints on his own man, but the policeman was being cautiously defensive—maybe waiting for reinforcements? Frank wondered.

"I can't quite get that . . . six bind," panted Rutledge. "How do you . . . take the blade to start it?"

"Watch," called Frank. He hopped forward, took his opponent's sword from below, and then whirled his point in around the other man's bell guard; he lunged, and the point punctured the eye and brain of the unfortunate Transport.

"Thus," said Frank, holding the position for Rutledge's benefit. "Begin it like a standard counter six. And finish with a moderate lunge."

"I see," said Rutledge. Frank straightened up to watch his pupil. After a moment the thief-lord leaped forward, caught the man's blade, and, lunging, spun his point into the man's eye. The Transport dropped like a puppet with its strings cut.

"Well done, my lord!" Frank nodded. "You see the advantage of practice. Now let's get out of this incriminating street."

Rutledge quickly dispatched the wounded policeman, and Bones, who had been sitting on a curb during the encounter, hopped up on Rutledge's shoulder. Lights had gone on and people were leaning out of windows, but Frank knew none of them would ever tell anything to any authorities. It was entirely possible, in fact, that the local citizenry would dispose of the bodies and weapons, leaving the Transport with, apparently, four more cases of unexplained desertion. Frank and Lord Rutledge strolled away down a cross street as casually as if they were leaving a poetry reading.

Frank escorted Rutledge home and then walked thoughtfully back toward Orcrist's dwelling. He was upset, but could not precisely say why. The killing of the four Transports tonight seemed stupid—not cruel or murderous, because those four officers certainly intended to do him harm—simply stupid. Why do I feel that way? he asked himself. Actually, it was quite a brave thing, two against four.

Brave? his mind sneered. You and Rutledge are superior swordsmen. You were safe. It wasn't bravery, it was showing off. You want to know what would have been a brave thing to do? To have pulled the trigger of Orcrist's gun, that night at the Doublon Festival. To have avenged your father.

All the sour black misery of his father's death and his own exile rose up and choked him. Tears stung his eyes; he clenched his teeth and drove his fist against the brick wall of Ludlow Alley. He stood there motionless for a full minute, leaning against the wall; then he straightened up and strode off, impatient with himself for having indulged this maudlin side of his nature.

When he entered Orcrist's sitting room he had forced himself to become quite cheerful. He poured a good-sized glass of scotch, took a deep sip of it, and then set it down while he fetched his pipe and tobacco. Orcrist had brought him a can of good tobacco, thickly laced with spicy black latakia, and he was beginning to like the stuff. Now he was even able to keep the pipe lit. Soon the pungent smoke hung in layers across the room as he absorbed himself with a book of A. E. Housman's poetry.

"Well, Frank!" boomed Orcrist's voice. "I didn't expect to see you this early. Didn't Rutledge show up?"

"Oh, he was there," answered Frank. "We broke up early, that's all. It's been an eventful evening. The Leethee, if you haven't yet heard, is *packed* with fugitive farmers from the Goriot Valley, all headed for the Deptford Sea—the south coast, I guess. And then on the way home Rutledge and I were stopped by four Transport cops and we had to kill them all."

"They were down here?" asked Orcrist. "Understreet?"

"That's right. Four of them, asking for identification cards."

Orcrist shook his head. "Something, I'm afraid, has got to be done."

Frank nodded and put down his pipe. "I've been thinking about it," he said. "The Subterranean Companions are a well-organized group, armed and more-or-less disciplined. What if we recruit and arm a few hundred of these homeless farmers and then overthrow the whole Transport-Costa government?"

Orcrist chuckled as he poured himself a scotch. "*Overthrow* is an easy word to say, Frank."

"But we could!" Frank insisted. "The Transports are having all kinds of financial difficulties—they couldn't maintain a long siege. And Costa is no military genius."

"No," said Orcrist, sipping his drink, "he isn't. But I'll tell you what he is. He's the blood son of Topo, and that's what counts. Even if we did, somehow, take over the palace and kill Costa, we couldn't hold it because we have no one with royal blood to set up as a successor. And that is a prerequisite. The citizens of Octavio may not be fond of Costa, and they aren't, you know, but they're bound up by centuries of tradition. They won't even consider accepting a duke who isn't of the royal blood.''

"Ignorant cattle," muttered Frank, aware in spite of himself that he, too, was unable to picture a duke who was not the descendant of a lot of other dukes.

"*But*," said Orcrist thoughtfully, "we might figure out a way to keep Munson Understreet, at least, free of Transport influence. I'll have to bring the matter up at the next meeting. Anyway, stop bothering your brains with politics and go put on a clean shirt. I've invited Kathrin Figaro over for a late glass of sherry.''

Frank stood up. "Righto," he said, heading for the hallway. "Oh," he said, turning, "I was just curious—I don't suppose there's any *truth* to George Tyler's stories about being Topo's son?''

Orcrist shook his head. "Come on, Frank. You've heard his stories. George is a good friend, and a moderately good poet, but a prince he is not.''

"I didn't really think so," said Frank, leaving the room.

Just as Frank reentered, buttoning the cuff of a new shirt, a knock sounded at the door. Frank threw himself into his chair and snatched up his pipe, then nodded to Orcrist, who proceeded to open the door.

"Kathrin!" he said. "Come in. You remember Frank Rovzar?''

"Of course," smiled Kathrin as Frank stood up and kissed her hand.

Orcrist took Kathrin's badger-skin stole and went to hang it up while Frank poured three glasses of sherry.

"There you are," he smiled, handing her one of them.

"Thank you. Was there a fire in here? I smell burning rugs or something.''

"That's my new tobacco."

"Oh? What happened to that wonderful cherry stuff you were smoking before? That smelled delicious."

"I think he lost his taste for it," said Orcrist. "Kathrin, tell Frank about your new job."

"Oh, yes. Frank, I've got a job in a dress shop on the surface! I'm a fashion designer. So you see you aren't the only one around here who can draw." Orcrist smiled wickedly and winked at Frank. "What were you reading there?" she asked, pointing at Frank's book.

"A. E. Housman's poetry," Frank answered. "Have you ever read any of it?"

"No, but I love poetry. In fact, I wrote a poem last week. Would you like to hear it?"

"Sure," answered Frank. "Bring it over some time. Would you like some more sherry?"

"No thank you. But I have the poem right here, in my purse." She rummaged about in the purse while Frank and Orcrist exchanged worried glances. "Ah, here it is." Then, in an embarrassingly over-animated voice, she began to read:

> "Love, called the bird of my heart.
> Do you hear it, the sweet song?
> The children go dancing through the flowers
> And I kiss your eyes like the sun kisses the
>   wheat."

After a moment Kathrin raised her eyes. "It's very personal," she explained.

Frank caught Orcrist's eye and looked quickly away. My God, he thought, I can't laugh! He bit his tongue, but still felt dangerously close to exploding. Picking up his glass, he drained his sherry in one gulp, and choked on it. He coughed violently and thus managed to get rid of the most insistent edge of his laughter.

"Are you all right?" asked Kathrin.

"Oh yes," he assured her, gaspingly. "But some of the sherry went down the wrong way."

"Well, what did you think of my poem?"

"Oh, well it . . . it's very good." Behind her Frank could see Orcrist doing bird imitations with his hands. I will not laugh, Frank vowed. "I liked it."

"I feel poetry should just . . . *flow* from the heart," she went on. "Do you know what I mean?"

"Precisely," nodded Orcrist. "Now, I'm an old man and I need my rest, so I'll be turning in. Why don't you take Kathrin for a ride down the Tirnog Canal, Frank? That'd be pleasant, and I don't imagine any of the Goriot fugitives would have wound up there."

Frank nodded, grateful that the conversation had been steered away from the subject of Kathrin's horrible poem. "That sounds good to me," he said. "Have you ever taken a boat ride down the Tirnog?"

"No," said Kathrin. "Is it safe?"

"Absolutely," Orcrist assured her. "Even if it weren't, Frank is one of the five best swordsmen in Munson Understreet, and maybe on the whole planet. You've got nothing to fear." He fetched her wrap, draped it about her shoulders, and surreptitiously slipped Frank a five-malory note. Frank got his coat and strapped on his sword and they were ready to go.

"So long, Sam," said Kathrin as they were leaving. "At least *Frank* doesn't run down at ten o'clock."

"I envy him his youth," smiled Orcrist as he closed the door.

Chapter 2

A night wind sighed eerily down the length of the Tirnog Canal, wringing soft random chords from the many aeolian harps and wind chimes hung from the low stone ceiling.

Kathrin leaned on Frank's shoulder. Frank put his arm around her—it seemed in some undefined way to be expected of him.

Paper lanterns, red, green and yellow, glowed everywhere, casting a dim fantastic radiance. By their fitful light were visible several ponderous, ribbon-hung barges rocking in the water, each one piloted by a tall, hooded gondolier who carried a long punting pole. Frank waved at the nearest boatman and the man pushed his barge to the padded dock.

"Passage for two," Frank told him, "to Quartz Lane and back."

"Two malories," said the pilot. Frank handed him the five and got change. He helped Kathrin aboard, and they sat close together on the wide leather seat in the bow while the gondolier pushed away from the dock. Frank trailed the fingers of his left hand in the cool water, and eventually put his right arm around Kathrin, who obligingly snuggled up under his chin.

Neither of them spoke as the barge drifted down the tunnel; the only sound was the soft bump of the pilot's pole as he corrected the barge's course from time to time. As the distance grew between them and the dock, the paper lanterns became fewer; soon they were in total darkness. Then, gradually, dim moonlight began to filter through cracks and holes in the ancient masonry that passed by over their heads, for Tirnog Canal, in several places, reached the surface, and the roof that had been built over it in such places was in bad repair. Some of the holes were a foot across, and the stars were plainly visible; and once Frank saw, like a thin chalk line across a distant blackboard, the luminous vapor trail of a Transport freighter hanging in the night sky.

Without premeditation Frank leaned over and kissed Kathrin, and was half surprised to find that she didn't object. Afterward she rested her head on his chest and he thoughtfully stroked her long brown hair.

At Quartz Lane, an abandoned stretch of once stately houses, the pilot laboriously turned the barge around and began working his way back up the slow stream, the thumping of his pole sounding regularly now, like a pulse.

When Frank got back to Orcrist's place he found a courier nodding sleepily in the easy chair. It was after midnight.

"Are you . . . uh . . . Francisco de Goya Rovzar?" the courier asked as Frank shed his coat.

"Yes. Why?"

"I have a letter for you from his majesty King Blanchard, and I've got to deliver it directly into your hands. Here. Now goodnight.'' Abruptly the courier put on his hat and left.

"Goodnight," said Frank automatically. Blanchard wrote a letter to *me*? He remembered his only sight of the old king, burly and white-bearded and gruff, at the first meeting of the Subterranean Companions he had attended.

He broke the seal and unfolded the letter.

> My dear Rovzar; I would be very pleased if you would drop round my chambers on Cochran Street this Thursday for the purpose of discussing and perhaps demonstrating fencing techniques. I hear from various acquaintances that you are very good.
>
> —BLANCHARD

Well, by God, thought Frank. It's quite the social climber I'm becoming. I'll show this to Orcrist in the morning. Right now all I want to do is sleep.

He put the letter on the table and stumbled off to bed. He woke up once during the night when a deep, echoing rumble shook the building; but it had stopped by the time he came fully awake, and so he just rolled over and went back to sleep.

THE next morning Frank put on his smoking jacket and wandered out to the breakfast room. The table was empty.

"Pons!" Frank called hoarsely. "Dammit, Pons! Where's my breakfast, you lazy weasel?" He knew Pons hated to be yelled at.

Orcrist entered the room. It was the first time Frank had ever seen him unshaven. Something, clearly, has happened, Frank told himself.

"What's up?" he asked.

"All kinds of things, Frank." Orcrist sat down and rubbed his eyes tiredly. "There was a demonstration last night on the surface, near Seventh and Shank. Shopkeepers or something, a whole crowd, hollering and demanding that Costa break all connections with the Transport. And from somewhere, God knows where, came flying an airplane with the Transport insignia. The damned thing circled the square where this demonstration was taking place, twice, and then dropped a bomb right in the middle of it."

"A *bomb*?" Frank was incredulous.

"That's right. Wiped out most of the shopkeepers, of course, but more to the point it tore a hole through four understreet levels, and caused collapses in five below that. The Companions alone have lost an estimated hundred members. Pons's wife was among the casualties."

"Pons was *married*?"

"Yes, he was. She went insane about four years ago and was committed. He put her in an old asylum up on Seventh; this explosion shook loose the roof of her cell."

"Bad business," said Frank.

"You could say so. Well then"—Orcrist looked up at him—"any news on the home front?"

"Oh, yes! There is." Frank went into the next room and got the letter from Blanchard. "Look at this."

Orcrist blinked over the letter for a minute, then put it down. "Not bad, Frank," he said. "I guess fencing has been your true calling all along."

"Maybe so." Frank stepped to the kitchen door. "Wait two minutes and I'll make some eggs and toast and coffee," he said.

"Thank you, Frank," said Orcrist. "Why don't you throw some rum in the coffee, eh?"

"Aye aye."

Later in the morning Frank went to see the crater where the bomb had fallen. He approached it from a little alley about two levels below the surface, so that when he stood on the alley's crumbling lip he could look down into a rubble-and-debris strewn valley in which workmen stumbled about, or up at the blue sky framed by the ragged outlines of the crater. Curls of smoke eddied up from the wreckage below, and fire hoses on the surface streets were sending arching streams of water into the abyss.

SIX men were in Orcrist's sitting room when Frank returned; they wore muddy jeans and boots, and had a wet, mildewy smell about them.

"Who's the kid?" growled one of them, jerking his thumb in Frank's direction.

"Partner of mine," said Orcrist, who strode in from the hallway, knotting a scarf around his neck. "Hullo Frank. We're going to go drop bricks on a party of Transport sewer-explorers. Want to come along?"

"Sure, I guess so. *What* is it you're going to do?"

"Oh, the Transport cops are puzzled by all the underground tunnels this bomb has revealed. They didn't know the understreet city extended that far. They'd be surprised if they knew how far it does extend! Anyway, they're sending exploring crews down into the crater to follow any tunnels they find and arrest whoever gets in their way. So we're going to go impede them."

"Yeah, I'll help."

"Good. Get a sealskin jacket and boots; there are three branches of the Leethee spewing around down there looking for new channels. And take a good hunting knife out of that closet. There'll be no room for swords, but there's always room for a knife.''

Frank quickly slipped into a jacket and boots and put a knitted wool cap on his head. Then, after selecting a sturdy knife, he was ready to go.

The eight of them left Orcrist's place silently and strode away down the low, torch-lit corridors. Bands of furtive, hurrying men were no unusual sight in the understreet city, and Orcrist and his companions caused no comment. They made their way northwest, filing down narrow walkways, going up and down stairs and walking along the sidewalks of big streets. These were areas unfamiliar to Frank, and he made sure to follow the others closely.

After about twenty minutes of walking Orcrist pulled them all aside into a little yard filled with garbage cans. "We split up here," he said. "Lambert, you come with me and we'll circle north and come in from the other side. Poach, you take Frank and go west around the crater. Wister and Colin, try to come up from below. Bob, you and Daryl wait here ten minutes and then go straight in. Everybody got that?''

They all nodded and broke up into pairs. Frank's partner, Poach, was a weather-beaten, middle-aged man with three fingers missing from his left hand. "Okay, kid," he said hoarsely, "follow me and do what I do." He had not looked directly at Frank yet, and did not now—he simply set off down the nearest east-west cross street. The older man had very long legs and a quick pace, and Frank had to trot to keep up with him. An uneven muted roar was becoming audible, and Frank knew it must be coming from the disrupted sections of the Leethee.

After a few blocks they took a right turn, which had them facing north, and Frank saw bright daylight at the end of the street; as his eyes grew accustomed to the glare he saw the jagged, tumbled wooden beams that were silhouetted against the brightness.

"This is it," whispered Poach. "Move slow and don't make no noise." Frank saw that Poach had his knife out, so he took his out too. He looked around, and realized that the last couple of streets had been completely empty. It's like sandcrabs, he thought. You dig a hole, let the sunlight in, and they all burrow deeper down, back into the darkness.

A harsh voice broke the quiet: "Tommy, get over here. They got more tunnels down here than an anthill." There were sounds of splashing footsteps and another voice, presumably Tommy's, spoke. "Captain, the whole floor is swaying on this level, and that damned river is thrashing around only one level below us. I haven't seen one person yet, and I say we should clear *out* of this lousy maze."

Poach made a "wait here" gesture to Frank and set off silently in the direction of the two voices. Frank stood absolutely still in the semi-darkness, clutching his knife and breathing through his mouth in order to hear better. Tommy has a point, he thought absently; the floor is swaying a little. A gray and white cat hurried by nervously, tail held high and eyes darting about. Frank tried to attract it by scratching his fingernails on a wooden gate post, but the cat, not in a playful mood, didn't stop.

A shrill, jabbering yell was abruptly wrenched out of someone's lungs a block away. "He's killing me, he's killing me, help me for God's sake!" Frank jumped, dropped his knife, picked it up again, and ran off in the direction of the desperate shouting. More yells echoed up ahead: "Look out, Wister, over your head!" "Not *me*, idiot!" "*Get* him, will someone once and for all *get* him?"

Frank rounded a corner, running as fast as he

could, and found himself in the midst of it. Two men in Transport uniforms were down and motionless on the street, and Orcrist was chasing a third, waving his knife like a madman. One of Orcrist's companions sat against a wall, white-faced, pressing his stomach with blood-wet hands. Two more Transport cops burst out of an alley at Frank's left, and one of them drove his knife at Frank's chest. The blade ripped his coat, but missed hitting flesh, and before the man could recover Frank drove his own knife into the Transport's side until he could feel the fabric of the man's jacket with his knuckles. The other one clubbed Frank with a blackjack in the left ear, and Frank went to his knees, dropping his knife. The cop raised his own knife, but Poach kicked the man in the stomach and cut his throat as he buckled.

Frank was trying to clear his head and stand up when the angle of the street pavement changed. He had fallen onto a level expanse, but by the time he struggled into a sitting position the street was slanted like a roof. Panicky yells echoed on all sides, so he knew he was not imagining it. The floor is collapsing, he told himself. That's the only explanation.

With a thundering, snapping crash the ancient masonry of the floor gave way like a trap door; Frank tumbled through a board fence, rolled over a collapsing wall and then plummeted through thirty feet of dust-choked air into deep, cold rushing water. The impact knocked the breath out of him and he was pulled far under the surface by savagely pounding whirlpools and undertows. Rocks and lumber spun all around him in the dark water, buffeting his ribs and back. Very dimly, he thought that he would not survive this. He convulsively gasped water, and then was racked by gagging coughs. Even if he could have mustered the strength to swim, he no longer knew which way was up.

He collided hard with a row of stationary metal bars. It must be some kind of grating or something, jammed across the stream, he thought. I could climb it and maybe get my head above water. *Why bother?* said another part of his mind. You've already gone through all the pain of dying—why not get it over with? You've earned your death: take it.

Working by instinct, his mind ordered his arms and legs to pull him upward against the wrenching of the cold water. In a few seconds his head was above the foaming surface and he was retching water, trying with desperate animal gasps to get air into his misused lungs.

He hung there for five full minutes, until the act of breathing did not require all of his concentration. Then he pulled himself along to the right, hoping that this gate, or whatever it was, was braced against the bank; there was absolutely no light, and he had to work by touch. A couple of times he felt the gate slide an inch or two, but it did not pull loose. Eventually he found his shoulder brushing against the wet bricks of a wall—that's all it was, just a brick wall with the rushing flood splashing against it. There was no passageway, so Frank simply hunched there on his perch of metal bars, with one hand braced against the bricks, and wept into the stream.

After a while he gathered his strength and began inching his way across to the other side, clinging tightly to the bars and trying to keep his body out of the water to avoid the wood and debris that were constantly colliding with the gate. Groping blindly in the darkness, he eventually found a rectangular opening that might once have framed a door. He managed to scramble into it and crawl a few yards up the passageway beyond. Then, free from the danger of drowning, he collapsed on the stone floor and surrendered his consciousness.

SOMEONE was tugging at his hair. "Lemme 'lone," he muttered. To his intense annoyance it didn't stop. He dozed, thinking, I'll just wait till they give up and go away. Suddenly he realized that he was cold, colder than he had ever been. I can't sleep, he realized. I've got to get blankets, fast.

He sat up, and heard a dozen tiny creatures scamper chittering away into the dark. Mice, by God! Eating my hair! "Hah!" he croaked, to scare them. He'd meant to yell, but a croak was all he could come up with. He crouched in the stone corridor, clasping his knees and shivering uncontrollably. I'm naked, he noticed. No, that isn't quite right. I've still got my boots on, and my brass ear is hanging around my throat like a necklace. If there was any light I'd be an odd spectacle.

He vaguely remembered his near-drowning and realized in a detached way that he probably needed first aid pretty badly. He stood up on knees that refused to work together, and staggered up the passageway, arms out before him to feel for obstacles. If I get through all this, he thought, I'll stay home the next time Orcrist wants to go on an adventure.

JOHN Bollinger was a religious man and took no part in the sinful society of Munson Understreet. He subsisted on fish and mushrooms and lived in a tiny one-room house that had belonged to his father. He had four books—a bible, a copy of *Paradise Lost,* the *Divina Commedia,* and Butler's *Lives of the Saints.* He always said, even when no one was listening, that to have more books than that was vanity.

He had heard the explosion during the night, but figured it was just a judgment on someone, and he forgot about it. He was looking at the Doré illustrations in his Milton when, the next afternoon, there came a knock at his door.

"Who knocks?" asked John.

There was no answer, aside from a confused muttering.

Rising fearlessly from his table, John strode to the door and flung it open. Confronting him was the strangest apparition he'd ever seen.

It was, as John was later to describe it to his pastor, "the likeness of a young man, naked and blue-colored. He wore curious shoes, and an indecipherable medallion about his neck on a string, and his hair was cut in a barbaric tonsure."

"What seekest thou?" gasped John.

"Clothes, for God's sake. Hot soup. Brandy."

"Aye, come in. Sit down. Of what order are you?"

"What?"

"What order do you belong to?"

"I don't belong to any order," Frank said. Seeing the old man frown, he added, off the top of his head, "I'm an independent. Freelance."

"An anchorite! I see. Here. You can use this blanket to cover your shame. Will you join me in some fish and mushrooms?"

"Will I ever!"

Half an hour later Frank was beginning to pull himself together. The food and strong tea that John had given him had revived him, and he felt capable now of finding his way back to Orcrist's apartment. I wonder if he managed to survive that street-fall? he thought. The last time he had seen Orcrist, he was chasing that Transport *away* from the collapsing street.

He must think I've had it, though. I'd better get back quick.

"Thank you for your hospitality to a naked stranger," he said, standing up and wrapping the blanket around himself like a robe. "I will repay you."

"Don't repay me," John said. "Just do the same some day for some other homeless wanderer."

"You bet," Frank said, shaking the old man's hand. "Can you tell me how to get to Sheol from here?"

"We all go to Sheol eventually," said John with a somber frown, "and we'd better be prepared."

"I guess that's true." Poor devil, he thought. Brain warped from a diet of fish. A lesson to us all. Frank crossed to the door and opened it. "So long," he said, "and thanks again."

It was chilly in the tunnels, and Frank was glad to have the blanket. He hurried southeast, numbed feet beating on the cobblestones, and finally did, as John had predicted, get to Sheol, where he turned left. He was wondering what he'd do if some understreet vagabonds were to attack him, because his strength and endurance were very nearly gone. As it happened, though, none did; he wasn't the type of wanderer that would tempt a thief.

After he'd found Sheol the rest of the trip was easy, and within ten minutes he was turning the emergency hide-a-key in Orcrist's front door lock. He swung the door open. The front room was empty, so he stumbled to the bathroom and began putting iodine and bandages on his various cuts and gouges.

Nothing seems to be broken, he thought, wincing as he probed a bruise over his ribs. Not obviously broken, anyway. His left ear was swollen and incredibly painful to touch, so he just left it alone. Finally he stood up and regarded his black and blue, bandage-striped body in the full-length mirror hanging behind the door.

Good God! he thought. What's become of my hair? He ran his fingers through the ragged, patchy clumps of hair on his scalp. This dismayed him more than anything else. Those damned mice *ate* it! I didn't know mice did that. What am I going to do? How can I face Blanchard looking like this? Or *Kathrin*?

He went to his room and dressed. He put on a wide-brimmed leather hat, tilting it at a rakish angle to keep it off his wounded ear. Finally he plodded wearily to the sitting room, poured a glass of brandy and collapsed into Orcrist's easy chair.

Chapter 3

Frank woke up to the sound of the front door squeaking open and someone scuffing mud off of boots. Frank tried to stand up, but a dozen sudden lancing pains made him decide to remain seated.

"Pons?" It was Orcrist's voice. "Pons?"

"Mr. Orcrist!" Frank called.

Orcrist stepped into the sitting room and stared at Frank in amazement. The older man was still dressed as he had been that morning, and still had not shaved, nor, to judge by his eyes, slept.

"I'll kill Poach," he said. "He swore he saw you and about two hundred feet of Henderson Lane fall into the river."

"Don't kill him," said Frank. "That's what happened. I managed to climb out of the Leethee after about six blocks."

"Are you all right?"

"No." Frank took off his hat.

Orcrist raised his eyebrows. "Why don't you tell it

to me from the beginning,'' he said, pulling up another chair. As economically as possible, Frank explained what had transpired after Orcrist ran off in pursuit of the fleeing Transport cop. ''Did you get him, by the way?'' Frank asked. Orcrist nodded. When the story was finished, Orcrist shook his head wonderingly.

''The Fates must have something planned for you, Frank.''

''I hope it's something quiet. How did the rest of you do?''

''Well, let's see. Wister and Lambert went into the river with you, and are presumed drowned. Bob has disappeared also. Poach is fine. I'm fine. You've lost your hair. None of the Transports seem to have survived.''

''What was the purpose of it? Just to nail some Transport cops?''

''No, Frank, not at all. What we did was . . . set a precedent. We've got to make it clear to the Transports that they are free to lord it topside, but have no jurisdiction understreet. If we can make sure that no Transport who comes down here ever returns topside, after a while they'll stop coming down.''

''Maybe so.'' Frank sipped his brandy. ''Is it inevitable that they lord it in Munson?''

''As far as I can see. Are you still thinking of overthrowing the palace?''

''Sure.''

''Oh well. A man's reach should exceed his grasp, and so forth. Would you like a wig? I'm sure I could get one somewhere.''

''No, that's . . . well, yes, maybe I would.''

DURING dinner there was a knock at the door, and George Tyler wandered in, grinning, leading by the hand a woman Frank had never seen. She was blond and slightly overweight; her eyelids were painted a delicate blue.

"Good evening, Sam, Frank," Tyler said. "This is Bobbie Sterne. We were just ambling past, so I thought we'd stop in."

"Sit down and have something to eat," said Orcrist. "Pons, could we have two more plates and glasses?"

"Oh, uh, look at this, Sam," said Tyler shyly, handing Orcrist a small book bound in limp leather. Bobbie smiled and stroked Tyler's arm.

"Poems," Orcrist read, "by George Tyler. Well I'll be damned. Congratulations, George, published at last! This calls for a drink. Pons! Some of the Tamarisk brandy! Sit down, Bobbie, and Frank, get a chair for George." Frank fetched a chair from the sitting room and took the opportunity to make sure his hat was firmly on.

"Frank," said Tyler when he reentered. "You're limping. And you've got a cut over your eye. Did one of your students get vicious?"

"It's the lot of a fencing master, George," said Orcrist. "Be glad you've got a more peaceful craft."

"Oh, I am."

Pons had, zombielike, served the brandy, and Bobbie was tossing it down like beer. Tyler took a long sip and smiled beatifically.

"Ah that's the stuff," he said. "I'll try to publish books more often, at this rate. Say, what do you think of that depth charge last night?"

"Depth charge?" Orcrist asked.

"Don't play the dummy with me, Sam. The Transport used some kind of depth charge to blow out ten levels in the northwest area."

"George, it was four levels, not ten, and it was a regular bomb. They dropped it on the surface to break up a riot. The only reason it did so much damage is that we've dug so many tunnels under Munson that it's like a honeycomb down here." Frank could see that Orcrist was controlling his impatience. "I think if anybody *stomped* really hard on any sidewalk in Munson a couple of levels would go."

"Well, maybe so," said Tyler, not quite sure of what was being discussed. "If I ever claim my kingdom I'll do something about it."

"That's a comfort," said Orcrist wearily.

"You think I'll forget? Just because I'll be living at the palace again? I won't forget old friends, Sam. I'll see to it that nobody stomps on any sidewalks over your place."

"Is this a limited edition, George?" asked Orcrist, thumbing through Tyler's book. "It's very handsomely printed."

"Oh, yeah, nothing but the best. It's limited to five hundred copies, and you can have that one. Here, I'll sign it. I'm not the one to say it, but it's likely to be very valuable in years to come."

"I expect it will," said Orcrist. "Thank you."

For a few minutes everyone occupied themselves with the dinner.

"You look tired, Sam," said Tyler, munching on a celery stick. "Been keeping long hours?"

"No longer than usual, George. I must just be—" he was interrupted by a crash from the kitchen. "Would you go see what that was, Frank?"

"Sure." Frank stood up and walked into the kitchen. Pons lay on the floor, unconscious, bright arterial blood gushing from a long slash that ran from his elbow to his wrist. Blood, spattered on the counter and wall, was pooling on the floor.

"Sam!" Frank shouted. He ripped his shirt off and

quickly knotted it around Pons's upper arm. Then he thrust the handle of a butter knife under the fabric and began twisting it to tighten the tourniquet. At the third twist the blood stopped jetting from the arm.

Orcrist ran in, stared at Pons for a moment, and ran out again. He was back in five seconds with a needle, fishing line, and the bottle of brandy. He poured the liquor all over the wounded arm, and rinsed his own hands in it. He then threaded the needle with the fishing line and began working in the gaping cut. "Got to try to repair the artery, you see, Frank," he said through clenched teeth. "There it is. Hold the skin there, will you?"

Frank held the wound open while Orcrist sewed shut the cut artery. Everything was slippery with blood and Frank didn't see how Orcrist could tell what he was doing.

"Okay, let's sew the slash closed now," said Orcrist, cutting off the line that dangled from the knot. Frank pressed the edges of the wound together and Orcrist sewed it up as neatly as a seam in a pair of pants. He released the tourniquet, and though blood began to seep out around the stitches, he declared that all was well. He used Frank's torn shirt as a bandage to wrap Pons's arm.

"Will that do?" asked Frank.

"Actually, I don't know," Orcrist answered. "It looks right to me."

Frank looked up. Tyler and Bobbie were standing in the doorway, looking pale and queasy.

"How did it happen?" Tyler asked.

"He cut himself, it appears, with that knife over there," Orcrist said, pointing to a long knife lying next to the stove. "When he fell he knocked over this cart."

"Good Lord. Should I get a doctor?"

"No, George, I don't think so." Orcrist went to the sink and began washing his hands. "I don't really think there's anything you can do here, so if you'll excuse us, Frank and I have a bit of work to do."

"Oh, sure, Sam. Come on, Bobbie."

Frank washed his hands; then he and Orcrist lifted Pons and carried him into his room, laying him on the bed. They heard the front door close as Tyler and Bobbie left.

Orcrist, looking eighty years old, Frank thought, sank into a chair. "This has been a day to try men's souls," Orcrist said. "You and I seem to have survived. I'm going to bed. We can clean everything up in the morning."

Frank stumbled to his own room, fell into bed and was plagued all night by monstrous dreams.

AFTER the grisly mopping up was finished next morning, Orcrist left the house for an hour. Frank spent the time reading Housman's poetry and drinking cup after cup of black coffee. When Orcrist returned he handed Frank a book-sized package. Frank opened it and lifted out the furry object it held.

"What the devil is it?" he asked. "A guinea-pig skin?"

"It's a wig, and you know it," Orcrist said. "Try it on."

Feeling like a fool, Frank pulled the thing over his patchy, bandaged scalp. "How's it look?" he asked.

"Pull it to the left more," said Orcrist. "There, that's good. How's your ear?"

"It doesn't hurt as much today. And I think the swelling's going down. Wait a minute, I've got to see how my brass ear fits with this wig."

Frank went to his room and took his strung metal ear off the bedside table. He put it on over the wig and it fit as well as ever, with the carved ear hanging exactly over the spot where his right ear used to be.

"It's a perfect fit, Mr. Orcrist," he said, returning to the sitting room.

"Yeah, you look like your old self. And I guess you can call me Sam, since you're not a kitchen boy anymore."

"All right." Frank sipped his coffee and wondered how one scratched one's head in a wig. "How's Pons?"

"He was conscious this morning and I gave him some potato soup."

"Is that what they give to people who've lost a lot of blood?"

"I don't know. It's what *I* give them."

"Say, Sam," Frank said, "was it a suicide attempt?"

"I think so. I wouldn't have sewed him up if I was *sure* it was."

"Ah." Frank stood up. "Well, I'd better be off to the school. I've got to start working this stiffness out of me before that appointment with Blanchard day after tomorrow."

"Okay. I may drop in later. I want some practice on that parry in prime you've been trying to teach me."

"Sure. You can even take over the lessons if I find I get too exhausted." Frank put on his coat and shoes, and left.

FRANK'S first pupil of the day was waiting in the street in front of the school when he arrived.

"Good morning, Lord Emsley," nodded Frank as he unlocked the door. "Sorry I'm late."

"My time is money, Rovzar." Emsley was a short,

surly man with a bristly black moustache and bad teeth.

Once inside, Frank lit the lamps and opened the streetside windows; the window that faced the river he left closed, since there were still a few refugees floating down the Leethee.

"Okay, my lord, take an épée and let me see your lunge."

Emsley selected a sword and crouched into an awkward on guard; then he kicked forward with his sword up.

"Extend your arm *before* your lead leg goes," Frank told him. "Otherwise he sees it coming. Do it again."

Emsley did it again.

"Arm first, my lord, arm first. And keep your rear leg straight. Do it again. And again. And again. Good. And again. And—"

"*Damn* you, Rovzar!" Emsley roared. "This is insane! There's no value in all these . . . *calisthenics!* Do you think it matters in a fight whether my leg is straight or my arm moves first? I'll tell you what matters: speed! Listen—I'll lay a wager with you. These ten malories say I can beat you, your style against mine."

The lord flung ten one-malory notes onto the floor.

"Okay," said Frank, picking them up and putting them on the table. "You're on." Dammit, Frank thought. I can't fence today. Every muscle in me is tight as a guitar string. But I've got to show this blustering idiot where he stands. Let me see, what are his weakest points? He doesn't parry well in sixte, when I come in over his sword arm. Let's see if I can do something with that.

"Here," he said, tossing Emsley a mask. He put one on himself and picked up one of the left-handed épées. God help me, he thought as he pulled on a leather glove. "On guard," he said. Emsley lunged immediately, and Frank parried it; but his riposte was slow, and the lord parried it without difficulty. Don't be lured into attacking, Frank told himself. Wait for another one of his stupid lunges.

A heavy knock sounded at the door. "Just a minute," Frank said, turning and raising his mask. Emsley drove his sword at Frank's back, and the blade flexed like a fishing pole as the padded tip struck a rib. The breath hissed painfully through Frank's teeth.

"You owe me ten malories, Rovzar!" crowed Emsley.

"Shut up, you ass," Frank said. He crossed to the door and opened it, and his heart froze. Three Transport policemen stood on the doorstep, and one of them, a captain, wore an automatic pistol in a shoulder holster.

"Yes, officers?" Frank said.

"Are you Francisco Rovzar?" asked the one with the pistol.

"Yes. Why?" Can I kill all three? he wondered. I don't like that gun. Emsley will be no help, that's certain, and I'm not in top-notch shape anyway. Better talk to them.

"Can we come in?" They were already walking in, so Frank nodded and bowed. "We stopped by yesterday, but you weren't here. We want to ask you about an incident that took place in the street two days ago. Did you see or hear or . . . do anything out of the ordinary on that day?"

"Friends of yours, Rovzar?" sneered Emsley.

"Who are you?" asked the captain sharply.

"Christopher Marlowe."

"Write that name down," barked the captain to one of the other officers. The man whipped out a

small pad and scribbled in it. "Now get out of here,
Marlowe. Rovzar, maybe you can explain how it is
that four Transport policemen were found killed in
the street two days ago."

"No," said Frank. "I didn't hear about it."

"Well, let me fill you in. They were killed in a
swordfight. Your fencing school is less than a hundred yards from the spot, so you're implicated. We've
come to take you topside for interrogation. Any
objections?"

The captain stood a good distance away, with his
hand near his pistol.

"Not at all," Frank said with a smile. "I assume
you'll provide lunch?" He hung up the sword and
mask casually. I could dive through the river window, he thought, but that would be a pretty clear
admission of guilt; I'd never dare come back here. I
guess I'll have to kill all three. If they get me topside
they're likely to see my tattoo and remember that
Francisco Rovzar who escaped from Barclay six
months ago. How long, though, can I keep killing
every Transport who wants to question me?

He turned to the officers cheerfully. "Lead the
way, gentlemen," he said. The captain strode out
while the other two officers seized Frank by the arms
and frog-marched him through the door.

"Take it easy, for God's sake," snapped Frank,
wincing at the pain in his arm sockets. Four more
Transports waited outside in the street, and fell in
behind the two who held Frank.

"Only one thing really puzzles me, Rovzar," remarked the captain over his shoulder as the grim
procession set off down the street. "Why didn't you
change your name?"

"Change my name?" panted Frank.

"Yeah. Did you think we wouldn't check? That

we don't keep records? When you jumped over the fence at Barclay and killed those two patrolmen, it was assumed that you'd drowned in the Malachi; but we didn't throw away your file.''

Frank didn't answer but cursed inwardly at his foolhardiness. I've had it. They'll ship me off to the Orestes mines, and it will be as if I'd never set foot in Munson Understreet.

A heavy sense of final doom settled over him, and he felt close to tears. He had to forcibly strangle an impulse to beg the captain to let him go.

They turned onto Harvey Way, and Frank knew they must be planning to ascend to the surface by way of the Baldwin sewer. His arms had become numb from his captors' tight grip, and he realized that the time to make a break for it, if there ever was one, had passed.

They had marched a hundred yards down the lamp-lit length of Harvey Way, the soldiers' feet clumping in unison like a monotonous military tap dance, when a sharp explosion sounded up ahead and the Transport captain abruptly sat down on the street. Surprised, Frank looked at the man, and saw blood runneling onto the pavement from a gaping wound in the back.

''It's an ambush!'' cried the policeman who held Frank's left arm, a moment before a slung stone cracked his forehead and he sprawled on the street. The other man released him in order to draw his sword, and Frank fell helplessly forward onto the sitting corpse of the captain. He heard swords clash behind him, but centered his attention on the task of getting his numb hands to pull the captain's pistol out of its holster. At last he fumbled it out, and rolled over so he could see the fighting. There were four Transports standing in a circle, fighting off about a dozen understreet brigands. Frank waited patiently until he had a clear shot, and then sent six bullets into the desperately tight police formation. By the time the echoes of the last shot had dissipated, several of the brigands had bolted in terror and every Transport was dead.

Frank dropped the empty gun and scrambled to his feet. One of the bandits thoughtfully fitted a stone into his sling, but a voice barked at him from farther up the street: "Drop it, Peckham. He's one of ours." Frank turned toward the voice and saw Orcrist step out of a shadowed doorway and wave at him with the tiny silver pistol.

"So it was you they were after, Frank! Come on, all of you! Down this alley here."

In spite of his dizziness Frank managed to keep up with Orcrist and his unsavory followers. They fled west, through several of the more dangerous understreet districts, to Sheol Boulevard, and soon they were all filing down the dark stairway under the sign that read "Huselor's."

Huselor's was a big, low-ceilinged bar, lit only by candles in glass jars on the tables. The floor was carpeted and the cool air smelled of gin. Orcrist led his band to a long table in the back, and they sat down silently, looking like a committee of especially disreputable senators.

Orcrist handed each of his hired swordsmen a one-malory note and they all stood up and exited, tipping their hats gratefully. Skilled labor is dirt cheap these days, Frank thought. That can't be a good sign.

When they were alone, Orcrist moved to a much smaller table and waved at a waiter.

"So, Frank," he said in a low voice. "How is it that those boys were leading you off so heavily guarded?"

"Two reasons. They're almost certain I helped kill those four cops the day before yesterday, *and* they know I'm the same Francisco Rovzar who escaped from Barclay six months ago. As that captain said, I should have changed my name."

The waiter padded noiselessly to their table and bowed. "Two big mugs of strong coffee," Orcrist said, "fortified with brandy. Do you want anything else, Frank?"

"Maybe a bowl of clam chowder."

The waiter nodded and sped away. Orcrist sat back with his fingertips pressed together. "That's bad," he said. Frank raised his eyebrows, and then realized that Orcrist wasn't referring to the clam chowder. "I heard, about an hour ago," Orcrist went on, "that a large band of heavily-armed Transports had been sighted down here, so I very quickly rounded up some rough lads, and even brought my pistol along, to go and . . ."

". . . set another precedent," Frank finished.

"Right. And it's a good thing I did. But if they've identified you that thoroughly, you can't relax yet. With the economy as shattered as it is, the Transport is able to buy informers very cheaply, and you never know which alley-skulker might be a spy or assassin."

"Great," said Frank wearily.

"It's tricky, but it isn't hopeless. You've got to go underground again—figuratively this time. Change your name, of course, and your location, and you'll be all right. But you'll have to move fast."

The soup and coffee arrived, and for a while neither man spoke.

"I think I've got a solution," Orcrist said, after five minutes of thoughtful coffee drinking. "I own a boat that's moored in Munson Harbor, just south of the Malachi Delta. It's very near the mouth of the

Leethee, so transportation won't be difficult. You could live there. It's got a large dining room below deck that I think you could easily turn into a fencing gym.''

"You think I'd still be able to give lessons?"

"Sure. The lords may complain, but they'll make the trip. I think they're beginning to see how much there is to know about the art of swordplay, and how important it is that we learn it before the Transports do. There's a crisis coming upon us fast, Frank, and *we* have to be the ones who are ready for it.''

Chapter 4

Frank paused in front of the dark glass of a shop window to straighten his wig and his shirt collar. He grinned at himself and walked on, swinging his leather case jauntily, his rubber-soled shoes silent on the damp cobblestones.

Cochran Street, a tunnel bigger, wider and brighter than any he'd yet seen understreet, lay ahead, and he turned left onto its uncracked sidewalk. The sixth door down wore a polished brass plate on which, boldly engraved, was the single name "Blanchard." Frank could feel eyes on him, and realized that he had probably been under several hidden guards' scrutiny ever since he'd turned onto Cochran.

He tucked his light-but-bulky leather case under his arm and knocked at the door. After a moment it was opened by a frail-looking old man with wispy ice-white hair, who raised one snowy eyebrow.

"My name is Francisco Rovzar," Frank said. "I

believe . . . uh, his highness is expecting me.'' The
old man nodded and waved Frank inside.

The floor was of red ceramic tiles, and the stark-
ness of the whitewashed stucco walls was relieved by
a dozen huge, age-blackened portraits. Candles flamed
in wrought-iron chandeliers that hung by chains from
the ceiling.

The old man led Frank down a hallway to a bigger
room, high-ceilinged and lined with bookcases. Standing in the center of the room, hands behind his back,
stood Blanchard. He wore light leather boots, and his
bushy white beard hid the collar of his tunic.

''Rovzar?''

''At your service, sire,'' said Frank with a courtly
bow.

''Glad you could make it. I hear the Transports are
interested in you. You know Sam Orcrist, don't you?
Would you like a drink?''

''Yes, I do, and yes I would.''

''I'm drinking daiquiris. How's that sound?''

''Fine.''

Frank leaned his sword case against a wall. ''Sit
down,'' Blanchard said, waving at a stout wooden
chair in front of a low table. ''I'll be back in a
second.'' He left the room and then reappeared immediately, carrying two tall, frosted glasses.

''There you are,'' he said, taking the chair across
from Frank and setting the drinks on the table. ''You
know, Rovzar, I'm glad you're on our side. Yessir.
Our boys were tending to get too smug about their
swordsmanship, and now they find out there's a
twenty-year-old kitchen boy who can beat 'em—and
give 'em lessons, too.'' Blanchard took a deep sip of
his daiquiri. ''Damn, that's good. The thing is, you've
got to be sharp these days.''

''That's true, sir.''

"You bet it is. I tell you, Rovzar, it's doggy-dog out there."

"How's that?"

"I say it's doggy-dog out there. The peaceful times are over. Peaceful times never last, anyway. And a good thing, too. They give a man a . . . rosy view of life. Hell, you know how I became King of the Subterranean Companions?"

"How?"

"I killed the previous king, old Stockton. I exercised the *ius gladii*, the right of the sword. It's a tradition—any member who invokes that right can challenge the king to a duel. The winner becomes, or remains, king. But don't get any ideas, Rovzar."

"Oh, no, I—"

"Hah! I'm kidding you, boy. I wish you could have met Stockton, though. A more repulsive man, I think, never lived. Do you play chess?"

"Yes," answered Frank, a little puzzled by Blanchard's topic-hopping style.

"Fine!" Blanchard reached under the table and pulled out a chessboard and a box of chessmen. He turned the box upside down on the table before sliding its cover out from under it. "Which side?" he asked.

"Left," said Frank.

Blanchard lifted the box and chessmen rolled out of it in two side-by-side piles; and the left pile was black.

"Set 'em up," said Blanchard.

Two hours and six daiquiris later Frank was checkmated, but not before he managed to capture Blanchard's queen in a deft king-queen fork.

"Good game, Rovzar." The old king smiled, sitting back. "I've got to be leaving now, but I'll send you another note sometime. Hope you'll be able to drop by again.''

''Sure,'' said Frank, standing up. It was only when he picked up his case that he remembered he'd come to discuss fencing.

THAT night Frank, wearing a false beard, plied the oars of a rowboat while Orcrist sat in the bow with a lantern and gave instructions.

''Okay, Frank, sharp to port and we'll be in the harbor.''

Frank dragged the port oar in the water and the boat swung to the left, through a low brick arch and out into the Munson Harbor. A cold night wind ruffled their hair, and the stars glittered like flecks of silver thread in the vast black cloak of the sky. The boat rocked with the swells, and Frank was finding it harder to control.

''Bear north now,'' Orcrist said. ''It'll be about half a mile.'' He opened the lantern and blew out the flame, since the moonlight provided adequate light.

The cold breeze was drying the sweat on Frank's face and shoulders, and he leaned more energetically into the rowing. Munson's towers and walls passed by in silhouette to his right, lit here and there by window-lamps and street lights. It's a beautiful city, he thought, at night and viewed from a distance.

''How's Costa doing these days?'' he asked, his voice only a little louder than the wavelets slapping against the hull. ''Does he like being Duke?''

''He's apparently trying to imitate his father, I hear,'' Orcrist said. ''Topo played croquet, so Costa does too, and his courtiers generally have the sense to lose to him.'' Frank chuckled wearily. ''And he's been seducing, or trying to, anyway, all of the old Duke's concubines. He pretends to savor the wines from Topo's cellar, but hasn't noticed that the wine steward is serving him *vin ordinaire* in fancy bottles, having decanted the good wine for himself. Oh, and this ought to interest you, Frank: he's decided he wants his portrait done by the best artist alive, just as his father did.''

''Hah. It's because of him that the best artist isn't alive.''

''True. And apparently he's not settling for second best, either.''

They were silent for a few oar-strokes. ''What do you mean?'' Frank asked.

''Well,'' Orcrist said, ''he's let every artist on the planet try out for the privilege of doing the portrait, but so far he's sent every one away in disgust once he sees their work. Your father seems to have set an impossibly high standard.''

''It doesn't surprise me. Art, like a lot of things, is a lost art.''

Orcrist had no reply to that, and just said ''bear a little to starboard.'' Frank could see the skeletal masts and reefed sails of a few docked merchant ships, and swung away from the shore a bit to pass well clear of them. Distantly from one of the farther ships he heard a deep-voiced man singing ''Danny Boy,'' and it lent the scene a wistful, melancholy air.

Just past the main basin Orcrist told Frank to head inshore, and in a minute their rowboat was bumping against the hull of a long, wide boat. It sat low in the water; they were able to climb aboard without paddling around to the back of the craft for the ladder.

''Moor the line to that . . . bumpy thing there,'' Orcrist said, waving at a vaguely mushroom-shaped protrusion of metal that stood about a foot high on the deck. Frank tied a slip-knot in the rope and looped it over the mooring, before following Orcrist into the cabin. The older man had just put a match to two wall-hung lanterns.

"This is sort of the living room," Orcrist explained; "and you can take that ridiculous beard off now."

Frank peeled it off. "It pays to be cautious," he said.

"No doubt. Through that door is your room—very comfortable, books, a well-stocked desk—and down those stairs is the dining room, another stateroom, and a storage room full of canned food and bottles of brandy. Don't raise the anchor or cast off the lines until I find someone who can give you lessons on how to work the sails."

"Right."

"I guess that's it. There are four good swords in your room—two sabres, an épée and a rapier. There's a homemade pistol in the top desk drawer, but I'm not sure it'll work, and it's only a .22 calibre anyway.

"I'll bring the rest of your things later in the week. If I can, I'll bring the swords and masks and jackets from the school." Orcrist took out his wallet and, after searching through it for a moment, handed Frank a folded slip of thin blue paper. "That's the lease verification. Wave it at any cops that come prowling about. And here are the keys. I'll leave it to you to figure out which lock each key fits."

"Okay. Why don't you . . . bring Kathrin along with you sometime?"

"I will." They wandered out onto the deck again. The moon was sitting low on the northern horizon now, magnified and orange-colored by the atmosphere. "Morning isn't far off," Orcrist said. "You'd better get some sleep." He lowered himself over the side into the rowboat. "Untie me there, will you, Frank? Thanks."

He leaned into the oars, and soon Frank could neither see nor hear him. Frank went below and checked the swords for flexibility and balance—the best one, the rapier, he laid on the desk within easy reach—and then went to bed.

THE next few weeks passed very comfortably. Frank read the books in the excellent ship's library, gave more expensive fencing lessons to many of the thief-lords (although Lord Emsley, by mutual consent, was no longer one of Frank's students) and frequently, wrapped in a heavy coat and muffler against the autumn chill, fished off the boat's bow. He often spent the gray afternoons sitting in a canvas chair, smoking his pipe and watching the ships sail in and out of the harbor. He had twice more played chess and consumed daiquiris with Blanchard, and been assured that it was "doggy-dog" out there. Orcrist was a frequent visitor, and Kathrin Figaro came with him several times. She found Frank's exile exciting, and had him explain to her how he would repel piratical boarders if any chanced to appear.

"You should have a cannon," she said, sipping hot coffee as they sat on the deck watching the tame little gray waves wobble past.

"Probably so," agreed Frank lazily. "Then raise anchor, let down the sails and embark on a voyage to Samarkand." His pipe had gone out, so he set it down next to his chair.

"I hear you've become good friends with King Blanchard," Kathrin said.

"Oh . . . I know him. I've played chess with him."

"Maybe when he dies *you'll* be the King of the Subterranean Companions."

"Yeah, maybe so." Frank was nearly asleep. "Where's Sam?"

"Down in the galley, he said. He's looking for a corkscrew."

"Well, I hope he finds one. Want to go for a swim?"

"No."

"Neither do I."

THREE miles away, in the low-roofed dimness of Huselor's, two men sat at a back table over glasses of dark beer.

"The thing is, dammit, we've got to keep it in the family. This kid's a stranger, untried, inexperienced."

"I'm not arguing, Tolley," said the other. "I just don't see what can be done about it right now. You could kill him, I suppose, but he's made a lot of powerful friends; maybe if you make it look like the Transports had done it. . . ."

"Yeah, maybe. I've got to get this . . . Rovzar kid out of the picture one way or another, though. What you heard *can't* be true—but if Blanchard *is* thinking of naming Rovzar as his successor, then the kid's got to go. I've spent years paving my way to that damned subterranean crown, and no kitchen-boy art forger is going to take it from me."

"You said it, Tolley," nodded Lord Emsley. "This kid is the fly in the ointment."

Lord Tolley Christensen stared at Lord Emsley with scarcely-veiled contempt. "Yeah, that's it, all right," he said, reaching for his beer.

ORCRIST stepped onto the deck, a corkscrew in one hand and a bottle of rosé in the other. He dropped into a chair next to Kathrin and began twisting the corkscrew into the top of the bottle.

"What have you got there?" demanded Frank.

"*Vin rosé*," Orcrist said. "A simple, wholesome wine, fermented from unpretentious grapes harvested by great, sturdy peasant women." He popped out the cork and pulled three long-stemmed glasses out of his coat pocket. When he had filled them he handed one to Kathrin and one to Frank. All three took a long, appreciative sip.

"Ah," sighed Orcrist. "The workingman's friend."

"The salvation of the . . . abused," put in Frank.

"The comforter of the humiliated."

"The mother to the unattractive."

"The . . . reassurer of the maladjusted."

"Oh, stop it," said Kathrin impatiently. "You're both idiots."

For a few minutes they all sat silently, sipping the wine and watching a fishing boat make its steady way toward the jetty and the outer sea.

"The guide of the lurching," said Frank. Orcrist laughed, and Kathrin threw her glass into the sea and stormed into the cabin.

"The girl's got a horrible temper," Orcrist observed.

"Only when she's upset," objected Frank.

Orcrist and Kathrin left late in the afternoon. Frank waved until their skiff disappeared behind the headland to the south, then went below and fixed himself dinner. He heated up some tomato soup and took it on deck to eat, and then lit his pipe and watched the seagulls hopping about on the few rock-tops exposed by the low tide. When the sun had slid by stages all the way under the horizon he went below to read. He sat down at his desk and picked up a book of Ashbless's poems.

An hour later he had lost interest in the book and had begun writing a sonnet to Kathrin. He painstak-

ingly constructed six awkward lines, then gave it up
as a bad idea and crumpled the paper.

"Not much of a poet, eh?" came a voice from the
doorway at his left. Frank jumped as if he'd been
stabbed. He whirled toward the door and then laughed
with relief to see Pons standing there.

"Good God, Pons! You just about stopped my
heart." It occurred to Frank to become angry. "What
the hell are you doing here, anyway?"

Pons took his left hand out of his coat pocket—he
was holding Orcrist's silver pistol. "I followed Sam
here," he said in a toneless voice. "I'm going to kill
you."

Just what I needed, thought Frank, *a maniac.* He
wondered if the gun was loaded—Orcrist had fired it
during that ambush a few weeks ago, and he might
not have reloaded it. Of course Pons wouldn't know
it had been fired.

"You're going to *kill* me? Why?" Frank furtively
slid open the top drawer of the desk.

"It's because of you that I've got to kill myself."

"Well, that's real sharp reasoning," said Frank,
gently feeling around in the drawer with his right
hand. "It wasn't me that put your wife in a second-
rate asylum with cheap ceilings."

"It was a good asylum!" Pons said loudly. "Your
bomb killed her."

No point in using logic with this guy, Frank told
himself. *He's gone round the bend.* At that moment
the fingers of his right hand closed on the grip of the
small pistol Orcrist had told him would be there. He
curled his first finger around the trigger and slowly
raised the barrel until it touched the underside of the
desk-top. He moved it minutely back and forth until
he figured it was pointed at Pons's chest.

"And you've got to die for it," Pons said, raising the silver gun.

Frank pulled the trigger of his own gun. There was a muffled bang and smoke spurted out of the drawer, but the bullet failed to penetrate the thick desk-top. Pons convulsively squeezed the trigger of *his* gun, and the hammer clicked into an empty chamber. For a moment both men stared at each other tensely.

Frank started laughing. "You idiot," he gasped. "Sam fired that gun a long time ago."

Tears welled in Pons's eyes and spilled down his left cheek. He flung his useless gun onto the floor and ran out of the room. Frank heard him dash up the stairs and out of the cabin; there were footsteps on the deck and then, faintly, he heard the sound of oars clacking in oarlocks.

Perhaps I wasn't as sympathetic as I ought to have been, Frank thought. Oh well; at least I didn't kill him. I'm glad it worked out as painlessly as it did. He thoughtfully closed the still-smoking drawer and picked up his book again.

THE sun had climbed midway to noon when Frank's first pupil arrived the next day. Frank sat smoking in a canvas chair by the rail and watched Lord Gilbert's body-servant maneuver the skiff alongside Frank's boat.

Lord Gilbert was a good-natured, very fat man, whose most sophisticated fencing style consisted of taking great, ponderous hops toward his opponent and flailing his sword like a madman with a fly-swatter. Thirty seconds of this always reduced him to a sweating, panting wreck, and Frank was trying to teach him to relax and wait for his opponent to attack.

"What ho, Lord Gilbert!" called Frank cheerfully. "How goes life in the rabbit warrens?"

"Most distressing, Rovzar," Gilbert puffed, clambering over the gunwale. "Transports keep coming understreet, and getting killed, and are in turn followed by meaner and more vengeful Transports."

"Well, doubtless they'll run out of them eventually."

"Doubtless. And now hundreds of homeless Goriot Valley farmers have settled, or tried to, understreet, and you know how crowded we were even before."

"True. What you ought to be doing, though, is training all those farmers in the arts of warfare, and then you should weld them and the understreet citizenry into an army to wipe out the Transports with."

"Yes, you've been advising that for some time, haven't you? But a farmer is only a farmer, Rovzar, and you can't *really* beat a plowshare into much of a sword."

"Oh well. Speaking of swords, let's go below and see how your parries are coming along."

"Another thing happened, last night," said Gilbert, stopping short. "Orcrist's servant, Pons, died."

Frank stopped also. "He did? How?"

"He walked into one of the methane pits near the southern tunnels and struck a match. I just heard about it this morning."

"Poor bastard. He never was a very *pleasant* person, but. . . ."

"You knew him, I see!" grinned Gilbert. "Come on, show me those parries."

Frank worked for two hours with Gilbert, to almost no avail. Finally he advised the lord to carry a shotgun and sent him on his way. Cheerful always, the lord shook Frank's hand and promised to practice up on everything and come back soon.

At about two in the afternoon another boat, wearing the insignia of the harbor patrol, pulled alongside. A tall blond man in a blue uniform climbed onto Frank's desk. "Afternoon," he said to Frank. "Are you the owner of this craft?"

"No sir," said Frank. "I'm leasing it."

"And what's your name?" The man was leafing through papers on a clipboard he carried.

"John Pine," said Frank, using the name he and Orcrist had agreed on.

"I have a Samuel Brendan Orcrist listed as the owner."

"That's right. He's leased it to me. Wait here and I'll get the papers for you." Frank hurried below, found the blue slip and brought it to the man.

The officer looked at it closely and then handed it back. "Looks okay," he said. "Just checking. Thanks for your time. Be seeing you!" He climbed back into his own boat, got the small steam engine puffing, and with a casual salute motored away across the basin.

WHEN Orcrist visited Frank again, late one afternoon, he brought an ornate envelope with "Francisco Rovzar, Esq." written in a florid script across the front.

"What is it?" Frank asked.

"It's an invitation to a party George Tyler is giving in two weeks. It's in honor of his book being published, I guess. He's invited all kinds of artists and writers, he tells me. More importantly, there'll be a lot of good food and drink."

"Do you think it'd be safe for me to attend? Where's it being held?"

"In George's new place, a big house about fifteen levels below the surface, near the Tartarus district.

Yes, it ought to be safe enough; the Transports never venture that deep, and no informers will be specifically looking for you, I don't think. Just call yourself John Pine and all will be well." Orcrist poked two holes in a beer can and handed the foaming thing to Frank. "I'd say you could even bring a young lady if you cared to."

"Good idea. Would you convey my invitation to Kathrin?"

"Consider it conveyed."

It was windy, so they took their beers into the cabin. "Oh, I've got something of yours, Sam," Frank said. He went into his room and came back with the silver pistol. "Here."

Orcrist took it and looked up at Frank curiously. "I noticed it was gone. Where did you get it?"

"Pons brought it here, the night he blew himself up. He tried to shoot me, but there was no bullet in it."

"Poor old Pons. Then he went straight from here to the methane pits, eh?"

"I guess so." Frank sat down and picked up his beer. "He said it was 'my' bomb that killed his wife."

Orcrist nodded. "Did I ever tell you about the time I took him along on a robbery?"

"No. You said you . . . gave him a chance to prove himself under fire, and that he didn't do well."

"That's right. It was about a year before you came bobbing like Moses down the Leethee. Beatrice, his wife, had already cracked up and been committed by that time, of course. Anyway, I decided to take him along on a raid on the palace arsenal; several of the understreet tunnels, you know, connect with palace sewers. Pons was extremely nervous and kept inventing reasons why we should turn back. Finally he worked himself into a rage and turned on me. He accused me of being in love with Beatrice and of blaming him for her crack-up.''

''What made him think *that?*''

''Oh, it was absolutely true, Frank. I was in love with her. I don't know why it was him she married—sometimes I think women secretly, unspokenly prefer stupid, mean men. But all this is beside the point. I called off the robbery then; it was clear that we couldn't work together. And that's the entirety of Pons's criminal career.''

''How did he become your doorman?''

''He had no money or friends, so I offered him the job and he took it. He and I had been friends before, you see.'' Orcrist's beer was gone, and he got up to fetch two more cans.

Chapter 5

Frank and Kathrin walked up the gravel path, their way festively lit by lamps behind panes of colored glass. Kathrin wore a lavender, sequined gown that emphasized her slim figure, and Frank wore a quiet black suit with newly-polished black boots. A dress sword hung at his belt in a decorated leather scabbard, but in the interests of security and anonymity he had left his bronze ear at home, and simply combed his newly-grown hair over the spot where his right ear should have been.

Tyler's house was a grand gothic pile, the roof of which merged with the high roof of the street. It looked as though it should have been a long abandoned shrine of forgotten and senile gods, but tonight its open windows and door spilled light and music into the street and up and down the nearby tunnels.

Tyler had been told about Frank's exile-status by Orcrist, so when Frank and Kathrin appeared at the door he introduced them to everyone as ''John Pine

and Kathrin Figaro.'' Frank then led Kathrin through
the press of smiling, chatting people, shaking hands
with several. They found space for the two of them
on an orange couch. He immediately took his pipe,
tobacco pouch and pipe-tamper out of his pocket and
laid them out on the low table in front of him.

''I sense wine over there to the right,'' he told
Kathrin. ''Shall I fetch you a glass?''

''Sure.''

Frank ducked and smiled his way to a little alcove
in which sat a tub of water and ice cubes surrounding
at least a dozen wine bottles. He spun them all this
way and that to read their labels before selecting a
bottle. He uncorked it, found two glasses and made
his way back to the orange couch.

''There we are,'' he said, filling the two glasses
and setting the bottle in front of them.

Kathrin sipped hers and smiled happily. ''I think
it's wonderful that you know a famous poet, Frank.''

Frank was about to make some vague reply and
remind her that his name tonight was John, when a
well-groomed, bearded man leaned toward them from
Kathrin's side of the couch. ''How long have you
known George?'' he asked.

''Oh, about six months,'' answered Frank. ''I've
never read any of his poetry, though.''

''He is the major tragic figure of this age,'' the
bearded man informed Frank.

''Oh,'' said Frank. He took a healthy gulp of his
wine and tried to imagine amiable, drunken George
as a tragic figure. ''Are you sure?''

''You must be one of George's . . . working-class
friends,'' said Beard, with a new sympathy in his
eyes. ''You probably never have time to read, right?''
He leaned forward still farther and put a pudgy hand

on Frank's knee. "*Can* you read?" he asked, in a
voice that was soft with pity.

"Actually, no," said Frank, putting on the best
sad expression he could come up with. "I've had to
work in the cotton mills ever since I was four years
old, and I never learned to read or eat fried foods.
Every Saturday night, though, my mother would read
the back of a cereal box to me and my brothers, and
sometimes we'd act out the story, each of us taking
the part of a different vitamin. My favorite was
always Niacin, but—"

The bearded man had stood up and walked stiffly
away during this speech, and Frank laughed and
began filling his pipe. He gave Kathrin a mock-
soulful look and put his hand on her knee. "*Can* you
read?" he mimicked.

"You didn't have to lie to him, Frank," she said.

"Sure I did. And my name is John, remember?"
He struck a match and puffed at his pipe, then
tamped the tobacco and lit it again. "I hope the
Beard of Avon there isn't representative of George's
friends."

"Oh, I don't know," said Kathrin. "He looked
sort of . . . sensitive, to me."

Tyler himself came weaving up to them at that
moment. "Hello, uh, John," he grinned. "How do
you like the party?"

"It's a great affair, George," Frank answered.
"By the way, I hear you're the tragic figure of this
century, or something."

"No kidding?" George said delightedly. "I've suspected it for a long time. Here, Miss Figaro, let me
fill your glass. Well, see you later, Fr—John, I
mean. I've got to mingle and put everyone at ease."

"Yeah, give 'em hell, George," said Frank with a

wave. Kathrin got up, spoke softly to Frank and disappeared in the direction of the ladies' room. Frank sat back, puffing on his pipe and surveying the scene.

The room was large and filled with knots of animatedly talking people. Bits of conversations drifted to Frank: ". . . my new sonnet-cycle on the plight of the Goriot farmers . . ." ". . . very much influenced by Ashbless, of course . . ." ". . . and then my emotions, sticky things that they are . . ."

Good God, Frank thought. *What am I doing here? Who are all these people?* He refilled his wine glass and wondered when the food would appear. There was a napkin in front of him on the table, and he took a pencil out of his pocket and began sketching a girl who stood on the other side of the room.

When he finished the drawing and looked up, the food had appeared but Kathrin hadn't. He looked around and saw her standing against the far wall, a glass of red wine in her hand and a tailored-looking young man whispering in her ear. A surge of quick jealousy narrowed Frank's eyes, but a moment later he laughed softly to himself and walked to the food table.

He took a plate of sliced beef and cheese back to his place on the couch; he had such a litter of smoking paraphernalia spread out on the table that no one had sat down there. When he was just finishing the last of the roast beef, and swallowing some more of the wine to wash it down, Kathrin appeared and sat down beside him.

"That's pretty good, Frank," she said, pointing at the sketch he'd done earlier. "Who is it?"

"It's a girl who was standing over—well, she's gone now. You'd better jump for it if you want to get some food." He decided to give up on John Pine.

"I'm not hungry," Kathrin said. "Did you see that guy I was talking to a minute ago?"

"The guy with the curly black hair and the moustache? Yes, I did. Who is he?"

"His name's Matthews. Just Matthews, no first name. And he's an artist, just like you."

"No kidding? Well that's—" Frank was interrupted then by Matthews himself, who sat down on the arm of the couch on Kathrin's side.

"I'm Matthews," he said with a bright but half-melancholy smile. "You are . . . ?"

"Rick O'Shay," said Frank, shaking Matthews's hand. "Kathrin tells me you're an artist."

"That's right."

"Well, here," Frank said, pushing toward Matthews the pencil and a napkin. "Sketch me Kathrin."

"Oh no," said Matthews. "I don't simply . . . *sketch*, you know, on a napkin. I've got to have a light table and my rapidograph and a set of graduated erasers."

"Oh." *A good artist*, Frank thought, *should be able to draw on a wood fence with a berry*. But he knew it wouldn't help to say so. Matthews now leaned over and began muttering in Kathrin's ear. She giggled.

Frank knocked the lump of old tobacco out of his pipe, ran a pipe cleaner through it, and began refilling it. *I'll be damned if I let them run me off the couch*, he thought. A moment later, though, Kathrin and Matthews stood up and, with a couple of perfunctory nods and waves to Frank, disappeared out the back door of the house. Frank lit his pipe.

"Not doing real bloody well, are you lad?" asked Tyler sympathetically from behind the couch.

Frank shifted around to see him. "No," he admitted. "What's out back there?"

"A fungus and statuary garden. Lit by blue and green lights."

"Oh, swell."

"Well, look, Frank, as soon as I oust my rotten half-brother from the palace, I'll have Matthews executed. How's that?"

"I'll be much obliged to you, George." Frank got up and wandered around the room, listening in on the various discussions going on. He joined one, and then got into an argument with a tall, slightly pot-bellied girl when he told her that free verse was almost always just playing-at-poetry by people who wished they were, but weren't, poets. Driven from that conversation by the ensuing unfriendly chill, Frank found himself next to the wine-bin once again, so he took a bottle of good *vin rosé* to see him through another circuit of the room. The glasses had all been taken and someone, he noticed, had used his old glass for an ashtray, so he was forced to take quick furtive sips from the bottle.

He saw Kathrin reenter the room, so he dropped his now half-empty bottle into a potted plant and waved at her. She saw him, smiled warmly, and weaved through the crowd toward him. Well, that's better, thought Frank. I guess old Matthews was just a momentary fascination.

"Hi, Frank," said Kathrin gaily. "What have you been up to?"

"Getting into arguments with surly poetesses. How about you?"

"I've been getting to know Matthews. It's all right with you if he takes me home, isn't it? Do you know, under his sophisticated exterior I think he's very . . . vulnerable."

"I'll bet even his exterior is vulnerable," said Frank, covering his confusion and disappointment

with a wolfish grin. "Does he wear a sword? Matthews, there you are! Come over here a minute."

"Frank, please!" hissed Kathrin. "I think he's my
animus!"

"Your animus, is he? I had no idea it had gone
this far. Matthews! Borrow a sword from someone
and you and I will decide in the street which of us is
to take Kathrin home."

Frank was talking loudly, and many of the guests
were watching him with wary curiosity. Matthews
turned pale. "A sword?" he repeated. "A woman's
heart was never swayed by swords."

"I'll puncture your heart with one," growled Frank,
unsheathing his rapier. A woman screamed and Matthews looked imploringly at Kathrin.

"Frank!" Kathrin shrilled. "Put away your stupid
sword! Matthews isn't so cowardly as to accept your
challenge."

"What?" Frank hadn't followed that.

"It takes much more courage *not* to fight. Matthews was explaining it to me earlier. And if you
think I'd let a . . . thief and murderer like you take
me home, you're very much mistaken."

Everyone in the room had stopped talking now and
stared at Frank. He slapped his sword back into its
scabbard and strode out of the room, leaving the
front door open behind him.

"HEY, Rovzar!"

Frank opened his eyes.

"Dammit, Rovzar, where are you?"

Who the hell is that yelling? Frank wondered. It
didn't sound like police, but it might well *bring* some
if it didn't stop. Frank rolled out of bed, slid into his
pants, grabbed his rapier and stumbled bleary-eyed
onto the dazzlingly-sunlit deck. A snub-nosed, insolent-

looking young man stood by the stern, dressed in close-fitting tan leather.

"Who the hell are you?" Frank croaked.

"I'm a courier. You're Rovzar, aren't you?"

"Yes."

"Well, here," the courier said, handing Frank a wax-sealed envelope. "Get some coffee into you, pal," he advised. "You look terrible." The young man hopped over the side into his own boat and began rowing away, whistling cheerfully.

Frank sat down on the deck and broke the seal. The letter, when unfolded, read: "Vital meeting of SC Tuesday at 9:00. Important announcement. Mandatory attendance unless specifically exempt by a reigning lord.—BLANCHARD."

Frank read it over several times and then stuffed it into his pants pocket. *Coffee,* he thought. *That's not a bad idea.* He picked up his sword, stood up, and made his unsteady way down the stairs to the galley.

"WHAT I heard was true I tell you, this is it."

Lord Tolley Christensen bit his lip, frowning thoughtfully. "That isn't certain, Emsley. Don't jump to conclusions." He stared again at the paper that lay on the table in front of him—it was a duplicate of the one Frank had received that morning. "Blanchard has got an 'important announcement' to make tomorrow. It might be anything—the Transport, the Goriot fugitives, the depression—it isn't necessarily the naming of his successor."

Emsley lit a cigar. "Yeah, Tolley, but what if it *is*? And the successor he names isn't you, but Rovzar?"

"You're right," Tolley admitted. "We can't risk it. Rovzar's got to be killed."

"Do it carefully, though," Emsley said. "You'll

be a prime suspect, and if Blanchard thinks you did it he sure won't make *you* his successor.''

"Blanchard won't have time even to hear about it, I think," said Tolley with a cold smile. "Have you heard of the *ius gladii*?"

"The what?"

"Never mind. Get out of here, now, and let me think."

TUESDAY night was racked with thunder and rain. Frank stood on the deck under the overhanging roof of the cabin and stared out into the thrashing gray rain-curtains for some sign of the bow-light of Orcrist's rowboat. The deep-voiced harbor bells and foghorns played a sad, moronic dirge across the water, and Frank's shivering wasn't entirely due to the cold, wet wind that whipped at his long sealskin coat. He waved his flickering lantern, hoping it would be seen by Orcrist.

Finally he heard "Ho, Frank!" from the darkness, and a moment later saw the weak glint of orange light wavering toward him through the rain. Frank swung his lantern from side to side. "This way, Sam!" he called.

A few minutes later Orcrist's boat was bumping against the bow. Frank climbed in, holding his oiled and wrapped sword clear of the splashing, three-inch-deep pool of water in the scuppers. He thrust it inside his coat and then took the oars and began pulling for the Leethee. The rain was whipping them too fiercely for speech to seem like a good idea, so the two men simply listened to the occasional thunderclaps and watched the rain stream off their hat-brims.

The boat lurched its laborious way around the ship basin and then turned in. After some searching, they found the arch of the Leethee mouth. When they'd rowed a hundred feet or so up its length they took their hats off and Orcrist began bailing the water out of their boat with a couple of coffee cans. The Leethee was deeper and faster than usual, and Frank was soon sweating with the effort of making headway.

"How well do you know Blanchard, Frank?" It was the first thing either of them had said since Frank had entered the boat.

"Oh, I don't know. I drink and play chess with him. Mostly he tells me stories about his younger days. Why do you ask?"

"Your acquaintance with him seems to have caused some jealousy in high circles."

"Oh?"

"That's what I've heard, anyway. Take that side-channel there, it'll avoid most of this current."

Eventually they pulled up to an ancient stone dock and moored their boat in its shadow. "Nobody's likely to see it here," Orcrist whispered. "Come on—up these stairs." Frank buckled his sword to his belt and followed the older man up the cracked granite stairs, slipping occasionally on the wet stone surfaces.

The steps led up to a long, entirely unlit corridor, down which they had to feel their way as slowly as disoriented blind men. At last they reached another stairway and found at the top a high-roofed hall lit by frequent torches, and they were able to move more quickly.

"Say, Sam, I've been meaning to ask you: was the Subterranean Companions' meeting hall ever a church? It sure looks like it was."

"Didn't you ever hear the story about that, Frank? There was a—"

A sharp *twang* sounded up ahead and an arrow buried half its length in Orcrist's chest. Frank leaped

to the wall and whipped out his sword, and two more
arrows hissed through the space he'd occupied a
moment before. Orcrist fell to his knees and then
slumped sideways onto the wet pavement. Six men
burst out of an alcove ahead and ran at Frank, waving wicked-looking double-edged sabres. Fired to an
irrational fury by Orcrist's death, Frank ran almost
joyfully to meet them.

He collided with the first of them so hard that their
bell guards clacked against each other, numbing the
other man's arm; Frank drove a backhand thrust
through the man's kidney. Two more blades were
jabbing at his stomach, and he parried both of them
low, then leaped backward and snatched up the fallen
man's sword. Two of the thugs were trying to circle
around him, so Frank quickly leaped toward the other
three with an intimidating stamp, his two swords held
crossed in front of him. All three men extended
stop-thrusts that Frank swept up with his right-hand
blade, clearing the way for a lightning-quick stab into
the throat of the man on the far left; whirling with the
move, Frank drove his blade to the hilt into a would-be
back-stabber's belly. The other man's blade-edge cut
a notch in Frank's chin, but Frank's right-hand sword
pierced him through the eye.

Frank backed off warily to catch his breath. Barely
five seconds had passed, but four of his opponents
were down, three dead and one slumped moaning
against the wall. Drops of blood fell in a steady rain
onto the front of Frank's dress shirt. The two remaining ambushers approached Frank cautiously, about
six feet apart. The man on Frank's right was leaving
his six-line open.

Frank tensed; very quickly he leaned forward on
his lead leg and then kicked off with his rear leg in a
rushing fleche attack that drove his blade into the

man's chest and snapped it off a foot above the bell guard. He spun to meet the remaining man, whose point was rushing at Frank's neck, and parried the thrust with his right-hand blade. Frank then drove his shortened left-hand sword dagger-style upward, with a sound of tearing cloth, into the man's heart. After a few seconds Frank's rigid arm released the grip and the body dropped to the pavement.

HODGES stubbed out his cigarette and stood up. The hall was full tonight—more members had shown up than he had known there were. Shouts and whistles and a low roar of talking were amplified in the cathedral-like hall until people had to cup their hands and shout to be heard.

Hodges glanced to his right into the sacristy and saw Blanchard, his hair and beard newly combed, give him a nod. Hodges banged on the speaker's stand with a gavel, but to no avail. He gave it a stronger blow and the head flew off into the crowd. Somebody threw it back at him and he had to leap aside to avoid being hit. He could be seen to be mouthing words like "Shut up, dammit, you idiots!" but in the general roar his shouts couldn't be heard.

Blanchard strode out onto the platform carrying a ceremonial shotgun, and fired it at the ceiling, where a few other ripped-up areas provided reminders of times in the past when this had been necessary. The sharp roar of the gun silenced the crowd abruptly, and the bits of stone and shot whining around the hall were all that could be heard.

"All right then," Blanchard growled. "Let's get down to business. The first thing we've got to get straight is—"

"The question of your successor!" called Lord

Tolley Christensen, who stood up now from his fourth-row seat.

"What's the problem, Tolley?" asked Blanchard quietly.

"There's no problem, sire. I'm just invoking a precedent—one you're familiar with yourself."

"That precedent being . . . ?"

"The *ius gladii*."

Hodges stared at Tolley in amazement, and there were shocked gasps from those thieves who knew what was being mentioned.

"All right." Blanchard raised his voice so that everyone in the hall could hear him. "Lord Tolley Christensen has invoked the *ius gladii* and challenged me to a duel. The winner will be your king. Here, two of you move this table out of here. Hodges, get my sword."

Lord Emsley stood sweating in the vestibule. He had posted six experienced, expensive killers in each of the three corridors Rovzar might have taken to get to the hall, and he had little doubt that Rovzar would be killed. Also, he had great confidence in Tolley's swordsmanship—still, he'd be happier when this evening was over.

Blanchard and Tolley now faced each other on the wide marble speaker's stand. They drew their swords and saluted; then they took the on guard position and cautiously advanced at each other.

Tolley tried a feint-and-lunge, Blanchard parried it and riposted, Tolley extended a stop-thrust that Blanchard got a bind on, Tolley released, and they both stepped back, panting a little. The assembled thieves growled and muttered among themselves.

Tolley hopped forward, attacking fiercely now, and the clang and rasp of the thrust-parry-riposte-cut-parry filled the hall. Tolley had Blanchard retreating, thrusting savagely and constantly at the old king. Finally a quick over-the-top jab hit the king in the chest; Tolley redoubled the attack and drove the blade into Blanchard's heart.

Angry yells came from the crowd as the old king fell and rolled off the back of the platform, and several of the thieves leaped up, waving their swords. Hodges, looking grim, raised his hand.

"There's nothing you can do," he said in a rasping, levelly controlled voice. "Tolley Christensen is the King of the Subterranean Companions. The only way to dispute that is to challenge him to a single combat. Are there . . . any members who want to do that?"

There was silence. Lord Tolley's swordsmanship was almost legendary.

"I'll challenge him," came a voice from the vestibule. All heads turned to see who spoke, and Tolley's eyes widened when he saw Frank Rovzar standing in the doorway. Damn that inefficient Emsley! Tolley thought furiously.

Frank shoved the gaping, pale-faced Lord Emsley aside and strode up the central aisle to the altarlike speaker's platform. As he approached he saw Tolley smile—he's noticing my bloody shirt, Frank thought. Good; I hope he overestimates the injury. He swung up onto the platform and nodded politely to both Tolley and Hodges.

"Did you hope to become equal to him by killing him?" he asked Tolley with a wild, brittle cheerfulness. "It didn't work—you're still a Transport-loving slug whom I wouldn't trust to clean privies." Frank knew Tolly hated the Transport as much as anyone, but wanted to enrage him. He succeeded, especially when many of the thieves in the crowd snickered at Frank's words.

"Ordinarily, Rovzar," Tolley said through clenched teeth, "I'd scorn to smear my sword with the watery blood of a kitchen boy. Since you're such an offensive and conceited one, though, I'll make an exception."

Hodges stood up and faced Frank. "Do you mean," he asked wearily, "to invoke the *ius gladii* against his majesty here?"

"Yes," said Frank politely. Cheers sounded in various parts of the hall. "Nail the bastard, Frank!" someone shouted.

Tolley, thoroughly angered, raised his sword and whistled it through the air in a curt salute. Frank unsheathed his own sword, the rapier Orcrist had been wearing, and saluted courteously.

"Go to it, gentlemen," said Hodges, sitting down.

Frank relaxed into the on guard position, with his sword well extended to keep a comfortable distance. He met Tolley's gaze and smiled. "It was you who hired those six bravos to kill me, wasn't it?" Frank asked softly, with a tentative tap at Tolley's blade.

"Emsley hired them," replied Tolley in a likewise low voice. "I told him to. I guess the idiot hired inferior swordsmen." Tolley tried a quick feint and jab to Frank's wrist; Frank caught Tolley's point and whirled a riposte that nearly punctured Tolley's elbow. They both backed off then, measuring each other.

"They weren't inferior," Frank said. "If they hadn't killed Orcrist before turning to me, they'd have earned whatever Emsley paid them."

Tolley backed away a step. "They killed Orcrist?" he asked, beginning to look a little fearful.

"That's right," said Frank.

Tolley took another step back, lowering his point—

and then leaped forward, jabbing at Frank like an enraged scorpion. His blade was everywhere: now flashing at Frank's throat, now ducking for his stomach, now jabbing at his knee. Frank devoted all his energy to parrying, waiting to riposte until, inevitably, Tolley should tire. He retreated a step; then another; and then felt with his rear foot the edge of the marble block. Desperately, he parried an eye-jab in prime and riposted awkwardly at Tolley's throat, leaping forward as he did it. Tolley backed off two steps, deflected Frank's thrust and flipped his blade back at Frank's face. Frank felt the fine-whetted edge bite through his cheek and grate against his cheekbone.

He struck Tolley's blade away and forced himself to relax and stay alert, to resist the impulse to attack wildly.

"You're on your way out, Rovzar," grinned Tolley fiercely. Frank drove a most convincing-looking thrust at Tolley's throat—Tolley raised his sword to meet it—and Frank ducked low, still in his lunge, and punched his sword-point through Tolley's thigh. He whipped it out and, grinning, threw aside the older man's convulsive riposte.

"Cut your throat, you bastard, and save me the trouble," hissed Frank.

Tolley stole a glance downward and paled visibly to see the widening red stain on his pants. Frank threw a quick thrust at him and cut him slightly in the arm. Blood was trickling down Frank's cheek and neck, and when he licked his lips he caught its rusty taste.

Tolley ran at Frank now in a fleche attack; the thrust missed, but Tolley collided heavily with Frank and they both pitched off the platform. As they rolled to their feet on the floor, Frank jabbed Tolley hard

behind the kneecap, and the lord cried out with the
pain.

"*Damn* you!" the older man snarled, aiming a
slash at Frank's head. Frank ducked it and Tolley
swung backhand at him again. Frank jarringly caught
the sword with the forte of his own and half-lifted,
half-threw Tolley away from him.

"It's time for the finish, Tolley," Frank gasped.
Sweat ran from his matted hair and dripped from the
end of his nose. "Have you ever seen the Self-
Inflicted Foot Thrust?"

Tolley said nothing, but lunged high at Frank,
hoping to catch him while he was still talking. Frank
carefully took Tolley's blade with his own, whirled it
up and then whipped it, hard, down.

Tolley crouched amazed, staring at his foot, which
was nailed to the floor by his own sword. Derisive
laughter sounded from all sides. Frank drove his own
sword with savage force into Tolley's stomach. "This
is for Orcrist," he grinned. "And this," he said,
with a punching slash that opened Tolley's throat,
"is for Blanchard."

Tolley's spouting body arched backward and
sprawled, arms outflung, on the floor. His sword still
stood up from his foot like a butterfly-collector's pin.

Frank sank exhausted to his knees and panted until
he'd begun to get his breath back. A minute later he
stood up, pushed his bronze ear back into place and
vaulted onto the platform.

"I present King Rovzar of the Subterranean Companions," Hodges called loudly. "Are there any further challenges?"

There were none. Lord Rutledge began clapping,
and in a moment the entire hall echoed to the sound
of applause and whistling. Frank grinned mirthlessly
and raised his bloody sword in a salute. Nobody

who'd known him a year ago would have recognized as Francisco Rovzar this savage figure standing above a multitude of cheering thieves, his uneven black hair flung back and his face a gleaming mask of sweat and blood.

BOOK THREE: The King

Chapter 1

Bright torchlight flickered on the faces of the seven men seated around the oak table. A nearly empty brandy bottle and a litter of used clay pipes gave testimony to the length of the conference, and one or two of the men were obviously stifling yawns.

"However you argue it," said one of them, obviously not for the first time, "you can't *hold* the palace. You might just be able to take it, as you suggest, with an army of thieves and evicted farmers. But without a prince of the royal blood to set on the throne, you'd be thrown out within the week and your army would be cut to bits and driven into the hills to starve."

"I guess you're right, Hodges," said the man at the head of the table. "We . . . shelve that idea, then. But you haven't given me a reason why you oppose the idea of night raids on the Transport shipment between Barclay and the palace."

"Well," said Hodges doubtfully, scratching his

chin, "I guess I don't really *oppose* it . . . but there
are two reasons why I don't entirely like it. First,
you're saying we should make a direct raid on the
Transport, which is bigger meat than the Companions usually go for. Second, it would be on the
surface, and our boys aren't used to working without
a roof overhead and a sewer or two to scuttle down if
things get tight."

"Well, our boys are going to have to *get* used to
it," growled the leader. "You know as well as I do
what that Transport last week whispered before he
died. Their home base, their system headquarters, is
what they plan to make of this planet. And do you
think they'll allow our little thieves' union to continue when Octavio is nothing but a Transport office
and parking lot? Not likely. We've *got* to impede
them, as seriously as we can, or we'll all be shipped
off to some prison planet within the year."

Hodges shrugged, frowning uncertainly. "That's
true," he said. "But the morale won't be good among
those who have to go on the raids."

The leader stood up and laid his smoking pipe on
the table. The scar of a sword-cut showed paler
against his pale cheek, and a glittering bronze ear
hung on the side of his head. *Quite a piratical char-
acter he looks,* thought Hodges, *but I wish he'd be
more realistic about policy.* "Would they feel better
about it," the leader asked, "if the man who led the
raid was their king?"

"You can't," said Hodges.

"Would they?"

"Sure. They'd feel even better if God led them in
a glowing chariot. But neither one is possible."

"Don't be so . . . hidebound, Hodges. I can lead
them, and I will. The next shipment of supplies will
be this Thursday night. I'll take ten of our best men

and capture the shipment; then we'll all have a late dinner and be in bed before one o'clock. No trouble at all.''

"It's a *very* bad idea," Hodges insisted.

"Most good ideas look like bad ones at first," Frank informed him.

THE moon was a shaving of silver in the sky, and Cromlech Road lay in total darkness. Crickets chirped a monotonous litany in the shrubbery beside the paved road, and frogs chuckled gutturally to each other in the swamps a mile to the east. The only motion came with the night breeze that swept among the treetops from time to time.

Frank crouched on a thick branch that hung out over the middle of the road, about twenty feet above the asphalt. He wore a knitted wool cap pulled low and a scarf wrapped around his face just under the eyes, and his sweater and pants were of black wool. His rapier hung scabbarded from his belt on one side; a long knife was tucked into the other. He was as motionless as the branch; even in daylight he'd have been hard to see.

Five men, also armed, hidden and silent, waited in the shrubbery on the east side of the road, and five more crouched on the west. None of them had moved or spoken for the last hour, and crickets and spiders had begun to build nests around their boots.

Frank stared at the empty stretch of the road south, only dimly visible to him, and tried to figure out what time it was. We've been out here about an hour, he thought, which would make it roughly nine o'clock now. About a half hour, then, until they come by.

Ten minutes later he tensed—a quiet, distant rattling and whirring was audible and growing momen-

tarily louder. He curled his fingers around his sword
hilt and waited, scanning the road more carefully
now. The sound, punctuated now and then by coughing or an interval of muted metallic rattling, eventually became recognizable: it was that of a man riding
a bicycle.

A moment later Frank saw the dim glow of the
bike's headlight; he could hear the man puffing now
as he pedalled the thing along, and he heard also,
very faintly, the long scratch of a sword being drawn.
Don't do it, Frank thought furiously. Can't you idiots
see that he's a scout, running ahead of the shipment
to make sure the way is clear? Frank held his breath,
but the bicyclist passed on by the ambush without
even changing the rhythm of his breathing. When the
sound had dwindled away behind him, Frank let out
a soft sigh of relief.

The shipment ought to be along promptly now, he
thought; and sure enough, he saw, dimly in the distance, twin pinpricks of light that could only be the
headlights of a Transport truck. He took a chance and
gave a low whistle to alert his men. They send their
scouts damned far ahead, Frank thought. We could
have killed that bicyclist easily, and even if he'd
yelled the truck is too far behind him to have heard
it. Or maybe the bicycle was wired with flares; if
we'd knocked it over, a dozen skyrockets would have
pinpointed the ambush and likely set us all afire.

The truck was closer now, and he could hear its
knocking motor labor up a slight rise. Well, Frank
thought, it's all in the lap of the gods now.

Nearer and nearer it came, until, when it was fifty
feet in front of him, two steel-headed crossbow quar-
rels flashed out of the shrubbery, both slanted to the
south, and tore into the truck's front tires. The vehicle was doing perhaps forty miles per hour, so the

stop, after the explosive loss of the tires, was a
screeching, grinding, sparking slide.

Frank had hoped the truck would stop directly
below him—it didn't, quite, so he dropped out of the
tree into the downward-slanting, dust-clouded headlight beams and with two blows of his dagger-hilt
smashed the bulbs. The driver and two guards leaped
out of the cab, brandishing swords at Frank, and
were cut down by arrow-fire from the bushes.

Frank whipped out his sword, leaped to the hood
and then to the top of the cab. Wooden boxes covered with a tarpaulin filled the truck bed; stretched
across several of them was the limp body of another
guard—apparently knocked unconscious when the truck
was stopped. Even as Frank watched, one of the
ambushers sank a dagger into the uniformed body.

Frank's men now dragged the four bodies into the
shrubbery while Frank climbed into the cab. He put
the gear shift lever into neutral, and his well-trained
crew pushed the crippled truck while Frank steered it
off the road. The massive vehicle was carried by its
own weight several yards into the bushes. Frank's ten
men cut branches from nearby trees and draped the
truck with them, and aside from the cuts in the
asphalt from the tire rims, there were no signs that
anything had happened here.

"All right," Frank whispered. "Quick, now, there
might be a scout behind them, too. Everybody take
one of these boxes and follow me. Forget the rest of
them—this time we'll take only what we can carry."

Each of the eleven men shouldered one of the
boxes from the truck bed and filed away eastward.
After about a hundred and fifty yards, they came to a
wider dirt road. Turning right, the party followed it
south for a quarter of a mile. Once Frank thought he
heard shouts behind them, but it was very faint. The

boxes were getting heavy and awkward, but no one spoke or even slackened the pace.

They finally reached the clearing where the eleven sleepy horses were tied. Frank and his men tied their boxes to the saddles, mounted, and galloped away east—a bit awkwardly and unsteadily, for none of them were really competent horsemen.

WHEN the last of the brigands had left the room, Frank turned to Hodges and the four other men at the table.

"Hand me that crowbar, will you, Hodges?" he asked. Hodges passed it to him. Frank pried up the nailed-down lid of the first box and lifted it off. In the box, wrapped in many sheets of waxed paper, were twelve .45 calibre semi-automatic pistols, glistening with oil. In the next box lay a thousand rounds of ammunition and twelve clips.

"Good God!" muttered Hodges. "Open the rest of them!"

Frank quickly opened the next box and found twenty rectangular sponges, rough on one side for scouring. The next box Frank pried apart held flat cans of saddle soap, as did the next two. Six metal bottles of kerosene lay in the next one, and the eighth box was filled with more saddle soap. The last four boxes held, respectively, handsoap, pamphlets on diabetes, a hundred fountain pens (but no ink) and more saddle soap.

Frank opened a drawer in the table and pulled out his pipe and tobacco pouch. "Well," he said, stuffing the pipe, "the guns and ammunition will be handy. Hell, all of it's handy in one way or another. These scouring sponges, now. . . ."

Hodges, who had been looking strangled, now exploded in helpless laughter. "Yeah," he gasped.

"These scouring sponges, now." He picked one of them up. "Nothing but the best. Duke's choice!" He picked up two more and began juggling them.

"For God's sake, man," said Frank. "Pull yourself together."

"Sorry, sire," sniffled Hodges, wiping tears out of his eyes. "It's been a long evening."

"For all of us," Frank agreed. "Now listen. We picked them off easily tonight, because they weren't expecting anything—their precautions were minimal and the four guards we ran into were just tokens. Also, the shipment itself seems to have been a . . . fairly minor one. It won't ever be this easy again."

"Right," agreed Hodges. "Next time they'll have a lot of alert, heavily armed guards riding along. So why continue? To corner the market in sponges and saddle soap?"

Frank held a lit match over his pipe-bowl and puffed rapidly on it. "No," he said, tamping it now. "Maybe you've forgotten those twelve pistols. And there are two purposes to these raids—to scavenge things for ourselves and to impede the Transports. And of the two the second is more important.

"Maybe you've also forgotten all those reports of construction going on in the Goriot Valley. They're building offices, barracks, factories for all we know! And when they're finished, more Transports will move in than any of you dreamed existed! How many times do I have to point this out? The Subterranean Companions will be a forgotten joke inside of a year. In the meantime, though, their supplies are being landed at the Barclay Depot and driven up the Cromlech Road to the palace or the valley. If we interfere with those shipments, we put off the day the Transports take complete charge of this planet."

"He's right, Hodges," spoke up one of the previously silent councillors. "It's the least we can do."

"Right!" agreed Frank eagerly, his bronze ear glittering in the torchlight. "It is the least, a mere . . . temporary cure. We have to, eventually, get rid of the Transport entirely, which means, of course, getting rid of Costa as well." He puffed on his pipe for a moment, sending thick smoke-coils curling to the ceiling. "We've got to find an heir—a prince."

"There *aren't* any, besides Costa himself, who has no children," said Hodges with some exasperation. "And you can't simply come up with a likely-looking pretender—you'd have to have documents, proof, things no forger could counterfeit."

"I can't help that," Frank shrugged. "That's what we need."

TOM Strand jogged up the steps of the Transport General Offices' building and grinned at his reflection in the front window as he straightened his tie. Ah, you're a bright-looking lad, Tommie, he told himself. He pulled open the door and approached the stern-faced woman behind the receptionist's desk.

"Uh, hello," said Tom shyly. "I was asked to come . . . that is, I have an appointment with Captain Duprey."

The woman pursed her lips and flipped through her appointment book. "You're Thomas Strand?"

"That's right."

"He's expecting you. Second floor, room two-twelve."

"Thank you." Tom found the stairs after a few wrong turns and soon was knocking on the door of Room 212. He was told to come in, did so, and found himself in a pleasant, sunlit office, facing a smiling man with gray temples and laughter lines around his eyes.

"Tom Strand? I'm Captain Duprey." The officer half-stood and warmly shook Tom's hand. "Sit down, Tom. Will you have some brandy?"

"Yes, thank you." Tom was gratified and profoundly flattered to be on such friendly terms with a Transport officer. *I hope I'm equal to whatever job they have for me*, he thought.

"Well, Tom," said Duprey, pouring two glasses, "you're in a position to do the Transport a big favor. And"—he looked up—"the Transport is not ungrateful to people who do it favors."

"I'll be . . . glad to be of service, sir."

"Good! I knew you were a smart lad when I saw you. I can certainly see we've picked the right man! Here, drink up."

"Thank you, sir." For a moment they both simply savored the brandy.

"Are you loyal to your Duke, Tom?" asked Duprey with a sharp look.

"Oh, yes sir!" Tom had, to be sure, his private doubts and dissatisfactions, but knew when to keep them to himself. "Absolutely," he added with fervor.

"Good man!" Duprey looked ready to burst with his admiration for Tom. "Now," he said, lowering his voice solemnly, "you were, I believe, a close friend of Francisco de Goya Rovzar?"

"Yes," said Tom, mystified by this turn. "He and his father disappeared about a year ago. I heard they were sent to the Orestes mines."

"I'll tell you what happened, Tom. They were in the palace when Costa overthrew Topo's decadent rule, and they resisted arrest. The father was killed and young Francisco escaped into Munson. You've heard of the Subterranean Companions?"

"Yes. They're the ones who've been raiding your supply shipments, aren't they?"

"That's right, Tom. Well, Francisco has become their king and is the instigator of these raids!"

"He's the king?" asked Tom in amazement. "Are you sure? How did he get to become king?"

"I understand he murdered the previous king, which is how succession works with these killers and thieves. Barbaric."

"It certainly is," Tom agreed. "I can see how he'd do well at it, though. My father is a fencing instructor, and Frankie was always his star pupil."

"Is that right? Yes, that explains a lot of things." Duprey flipped open a wooden box on his desk. "Have a cigar, Tom," he said. "Genuine Havanas, all the way from Earth."

Tom took a cigar, glorying in his apparent equality with this space-wise, experienced old soldier. Duprey lit it for him, and Tom puffed at it with an expression of determined enjoyment.

"This brings us right to the point," Duprey went on. "I won't mince words, for I see you're a man who likes to know straight-out what's what. Frank Rovzar is a criminal and a leader of other criminals. He is almost certainly responsible for the deaths of . . . let's see . . . eighteen Transport soldiers, several of them officers, and his raids on our shipments are becoming more costly all the time. You see the position he puts us in?"

"I certainly do, sir."

"Good. Now what I . . . what the Transport asks of you is that you enlist in the Subterranean Companions. We'll provide you with a credible story, of course. Then you can pretend to reestablish your friendship with him; get close to him; and then, quickly and mercifully, execute him. You'll be acting as a representative of the state, naturally, and when you return from this valuable mission you'll be given a high position in our company—as well as a cash reward for Rovzar's death. It's a fairly dangerous adventure, I know, and many men would fear to take opportunity's somewhat bloody hand. But, unless I'm mistaken, you're made of sterner stuff.''

Tom gulped his brandy, trying hard to mask the uncertainty inside him. Even for a high position in the Transport, he thought, can I coldly kill old Frank? Still, if I turn Duprey down I'll likely wind up in jail myself.

"I'm always ready to do my country's bidding,'' Tom said with a pious look. "I'll do my best, sir.''

"I knew you were our man!'' said Duprey with the sort of smile one saves for a true comrade.

UNLIKE Blanchard, Frank made it a point to attend as many meetings of the Subterranean Companions as he could. He liked to keep up on the news and to learn as much as possible about the workings of the organization he'd become king of. Generally he sat to the side, smoking thoughtfully, only occasionally speaking up to add something or ask a question of Hodges.

Tonight he squinted curiously through a haze of latakia smoke at Hodges, who had just claimed to have an announcement to make about "the deceased king, Tolley Christensen.''

"After the duel in which Tolley Christensen was killed,'' Hodges read from his notes, "his sword was picked up, together with the sword of King Blanchard. The two swords were observed to cling to each other. Upon investigation, Tolley's sword proved to be magnetized. This is a trick expressly forbidden in the bylaws, and therefore I declare that Tolley's admittedly brief reign was won by unfair means, and is, because of that, invalidated. Henceforth, then, our

present King Francisco Rovzar is to be remembered
as the successor to King Blanchard, with none
between.''

Frank felt a quick panic. That means that Tolley
wasn't king when I killed him, he thought. Therefore, technically, I'm not really the king now. Damn
it, Hodges, I wish you'd cleared this with me before
announcing it.

Oh hell, he thought. Even if they do appoint someone else, I can always pull the *ius gladii* out of the
hat again. And they'll know I will, so they won't try
it even if they think of it.

A magnetized sword, eh, Tolley? Were you that
scared of Blanchard? In the legendry and superstition
of the understreet thieves, a magnetized sword was
reputed to be much deadlier than an ordinary one; but
Frank couldn't see that it would make any difference.
It just might, he thought, make getting a bind a little
easier, and it might make your parries a little quicker—
but it would do the same for your opponent, too.

Frank suddenly snapped out of his revery. Hodges
was now reading the names of newly bonded apprentices. ''What was that last name, Hodges?''

''Uh . . . Thomas Strand.''

''Thank you.''

Thomas Strand! Could it be my old buddy? Frank
wondered. I'll have to check the lists after the meeting and see where this Strand is staying. It would be
great to have Tom down here. Since Orcrist was
killed, I don't have a really close friend in this
understreet antfarm—only George Tyler, I guess; and
maybe Beardo Jackson.

Eventually Hodges declared the meeting adjourned,
and the crowd broke up into departing groups arguing
about where to go for beer. Hodges was shuffling his
papers together and a handful of young apprentices

were waiting for the nod to drag out the ladders and snuff the lights.

"Hodges," Frank said. "I think I know one of the new apprentices. Let me—"

"Frank!" came a voice from below him. "Your majesty, I mean."

Frank looked down and grinned to see Tom Strand standing in front of the first-row seats. Frank jumped down from the marble block and slapped him on the back. "When the hell did you fall into the sewer world, Tom?"

"A couple of days ago. I saw you kind of blink when the emcee read my name. But Frank, you look ten years older! You've got a metal ear! And how did you cut your face? Shaving?"

"We've both got long stories to tell, I'm sure. I'm taking off, Hodges. Oh, and I'd like to see you tomorrow at ten in the council room; there's a detail or two of protocol I want to check with you on."

"Right, sire." Hodges leaped down from the platform and ambled into the sacristy.

"Come on," Frank said. "I know where we can get some beer." As they walked out he waved to the boys, who trudged off to the closet where the ladders were kept.

"TOLLEY killed Orcrist and Blanchard, both of them friends of mine, so I killed him. Afterward I found that that had made me the new king. And here I am. So how is it that you've become one of my subjects?"

Tom mentally ran through the story Duprey had provided him with. "Well, Frank, my old girlfriend, Bonnie—remember her? Of course you do—Bonnie and I were out getting drunk one night, and a Transport cop came over and said to her 'Drop creepo, here, baby, and try a *real* man.' Well, I told him to, you know, buzz off, and he punched me in the face, so I hit him with a bottle and he fell right over, like he was dead.''

He's lying, Frank thought—or at least exaggerating. Oh well, if he wants to look brave, I won't hinder him.

"There were about six other Transports there, and they went for me, swords out. I've never been scared by swords, you know that, but I figured six of 'em were too many, so I headed out the door.''

"What about Bonnie?''

"Hm?''

"Bonnie. You left her there?''

"Oh . . . no, no. I knew the guy that owned the place, see, and I knew he'd look after her. Anyway, I ran out of there and headed for Munson. I didn't have any place to stay, and Munson in the winter isn't the right town for sidewalk-sleeping, so I crawled into a sewer, followed it along, and found a whole city down here.''

"You were lucky you did. Munson on the surface is a Transport nest. Who's your sponsor?''

"An old guy named Jack Plant. Know him?''

"Slightly.'' Frank frowned inwardly. Plant was a perpetual whiner and complainer, and had in the past been vaguely suspected of having made deals with the surface police. "I'll get you a good position so you can pay off your bond quickly.''

"Thanks, Frank. But I don't want you doing me favors just because I'm your friend.''

"Don't worry. I never let personal feelings interfere with what's got to be done. But getting you a job isn't any trouble. Finish your beer, now, and I'll show you the way back to Plant's.''

After Frank had left, Tom sat drinking weak coffee in Plant's front room. I can't kill old Frank, Tom thought, even if he is a criminal. The poor devil's had a horrible time and has to live his whole life underground in a sewer. Of course it isn't *that* bad— and he's living high, by sewer standards.

Maybe, Tom thought, I could *pretend* to kill him. I could buy a slave of roughly Frank's build, and then cut the slave's head off and dress him in Frank's clothes and tell Duprey that it was Frank. Then I'd have to do something with Frank . . . maybe I could sell him into slavery in the Tamarisk Isles. I'd have to cut out his tongue, I suppose, but that's better than being killed. I guess it would probably be best to blind him, too—can't have him coming back, after all—but that's *still* better than being killed.

Tom was gratified to see how readily he could think in these harsh terms.

Yessir, Tom smiled to himself, that's what I'll do. That way I get the Transport post Duprey promised me, and I don't have to kill Frank. Hell, he'll probably be happier, dumb and blind in the sunny Tamarisk Isles.

"OKAY, Hodges, that wasn't it. Send in the next one." Frank leaned back in his chair and wished he had his pipe.

The door opened and a thin, well-dressed man entered the room. His suit was clean and meticulously pressed, but looked a bit threadbare around the cuffs. He had apparently combed his hair recently with some kind of oil.

"Please sit down," said Frank. "You are related to the royal family, I believe?"

"That's right," the man nodded.

"What is your connection?"

"My father was the rightful duke, and Topo had him killed so he could marry my mother."

"Your father was Duke Ovidi?" Frank asked.

"That's right. Topo had him killed."

"How?" Frank had always understood that Ovidi had died after falling, drunk, down a flight of stairs, thus leaving the dukedom to his brother Topo.

"My father was sleeping, and two scoundrels that Topo had hired snuck up and poured poison in his ear. Then Topo married my mother and took the title of Duke. But now I think it's time that I claimed my kinship and threw Topo out. I've been having visions—"

"Yes, yes," said Frank hastily. "Visions. I see. Well, thank you for your time. If anything develops, we'll get in touch with you."

The man stood up uncertainly and ambled out of the room. A moment later Hodges leaned in. "Another blank?" he asked.

Frank nodded.

"Nut or fortune-hunter?"

"Nut, for sure," said Frank. "The guy doesn't know Topo's dead, even."

"Well, I've got six more out here. You want 'em now or save 'em to see tomorrow?"

"Oh, tomorrow, I guess. We've *got* to find an heir, Hodges."

"If you say so, sire."

Frank waited until Hodges had got rid of the six other pretenders to the throne, and then went downstairs and put on his coat and sword.

"Going somewhere, sire?" Hodges asked.

"Yeah; I'm meeting a couple of friends on the boat."

"Be careful."

"Always, Hodges."

Cochran Street was empty as Frank closed the door behind him. The air was chilly, and foul with fumes that were filtering up from some low-level swamp or stagnant branch of the Leethee. He pulled his coat tighter about him and strode off rapidly toward his dock. After insisting that his boatman and two guards remain where they were, Frank untied a small rowboat and took off down the Leethee. The river was flowing quick and smooth, but the choppy water and erratic evening wind of the harbor slowed him down. When he reached the anchored boat another rowboat was already moored to it.

"Frank!" someone called from the deck. "Get up here with the key, for God's sake!"

Frank tied his rowboat to a mooring ring and climbed aboard the larger vessel. George Tyler stood shivering on the afterdeck, clutching a wine bottle as if it were a threatened baby. Frank unlocked the cabin and they both hurried inside.

"Get the heater lit," gasped Tyler. "I've been out there for an hour."

"You have not."

"Well, nearly. Who's this friend I've got to meet?"

"His name's Tom Strand. He was my best friend before I came understreet."

"Oh." Tyler struck a match and lit the lamps. "Say, Frank, I'm sorry about what happened at my party."

"Forget it, George. I'd say Kathrin and that Matthews dimwit are made for each other."

"I guess so. They certainly see a lot of each other, anyway." Tyler slumped into a chair. "Say," he said, "where is Sam's grave? I never thought to ask, but now I'd like to go and . . . pour some wine on his last resting place, or something."

"He doesn't have a grave," Frank told him.

"You didn't bury him?"

Frank pulled the cork out of George's wine bottle. "Not exactly. I dragged his body back to our boat and then went on to that meeting we'd been heading for. Afterward I rowed out past the jetty and tied a heavy chain around him and let him sink in the outer sea." He handed Tyler a glass of wine.

Tyler frowned for a moment, and then nodded. "You did the right thing, Frank. Bodies buried understreet always pop out sooner or later on a lower level. Here's to his shade!" He tossed off the wine.

Frank drained his, too, and flung the glass hard at the narrow starboard window, which shattered explosively outward, spraying the deck with tinkling glass. Tyler flung his through the jagged hole into the sea.

"Hey, take it easy!" someone called from outside. "Frank, is that you?"

"That must be Tom," Frank said, walking to the door. "I was beginning to worry about him."

Frank went out on deck and showed Tom where to tie his boat, then helped him aboard and opened the cabin door for him.

(Two hundred yards away a tall, blond man in the harbor patrol uniform lowered his binoculars. He looked pleased as he took up the oars and began pulling toward the south.)

"This is George Tyler, Tom, one of the great poets of our age," Frank said. "George, this is Tom Strand. Will you have some wine, Tom?"

"Sure. I can never afford any on an apprentice's wages."

"Maybe you can do better than that," said Frank, pouring two new glasses for Tyler and himself. "I have a position for you."

"Oh?" Tom took his glass and sat down. "Doing what?"

"Training my troops in fencing. They—"

"*Troops*?" Tom asked incredulously.

"That's right. I've been organizing these thieves and a lot of the homeless Goriot farmers into an army. I'm beginning to get them into some kind of shape, but they know nothing about real fighting. I've been giving groups of them some basic lessons in stance and parrying and all, but I need someone who can be a full-time instructor. You're probably as good a fencer as I am; why don't you take the job? You'll have your bond paid off in no time."

Tom stared into his wine. *An underground army,* he thought. Duprey will be damned grateful when I tell him. "Sure," he answered, looking up. "It sounds fine to me."

"Terrific. You can start the day after tomorrow. I'll have Hodges get a group of the best ones together in the meeting hall."

They soon finished the wine and opened a bottle of Tamarisk brandy; the sight brought tears to Tom's eyes.

"Easy, Tom," Frank said jovially. "I guess it's been a long time since you've had good brandy. Relax. Real soon you'll be able to buy all the fine brandy you want."

"I know," said Tom.

Chapter 2

A fly was circling, in the aimless way of flies, in and out of a beam of morning sunlight in Duke Costa's throne room, annoying him mightily. Three hard-eyed, leather-faced men stood in front of him and watched impassively as the powdered and jewel-decked Duke flung books at the insect.

Finally one of them spoke. "Your grace," he rasped. "Why have you called for us?"

"What? Oh. You're the assassins, right?"

The three men exchanged cold looks. "We served your father in many ways," said another of them.

"I know. But right now it's only as assassins that I want to see you. Now listen closely, I hate repeating myself. The King of the Subterranean Companions is a young man named Francisco Rovzar. He owns a large boat in the harbor, just north of the ship basin, and he spends time there, I've heard, when he wants to relax after doing whatever horrible things he does—interfering with the government, mostly. Anyway, I

want you to kill him. I'll pay you the same rate my
father did.''

"Double it," growled one. "The malory isn't worth
a sowbug's dowry these days.''

Costa frowned and pressed his lips together, but
nodded. The three men bowed and filed out of the
room.

They're insolent boys, Costa thought. I probably
should have had them seized and flung into a dun-
geon (I wonder if I have any dungeons?). But no, I'll
let them kill Rovzar first. It will be fun to mention,
off the cuff, of course, to those serious-minded Transports that I've succeeded where they've failed, and
had Rovzar killed without their tiresome help.

TOM Strand lifted his mask so that it sat on his
head like a conquistador's helmet. "Okay," he called
to the thirty sweating men lined up in the hall. "Advance, advance, advance, retreat, advance, *lunge*!''
His students leaped about awkwardly, thrusting their
swords in all directions. "Well, that's pretty bad,"
Tom said. "Let's call it a day. But be back here
tomorrow—I'll teach this stuff to you guys or kill
you all trying.''

The thirty thieves sheathed their swords and swag-
gered out of the hall, clearly pleased with themselves. Tom threw his mask onto the floor, sheathed
his own sword and hurried out after them. He decided he didn't have time to change out of his white
fencing clothes.

He made his furtive way down a little-used alley
that opened onto a stairway, which he followed down
two flights. Moored to an ancient stone dock was a
small skiff, in the bottom of which lay two oars, a
wide-bladed axe and a bound and gagged man. Tom

hopped in, shoved the tied man aside, loosed the rope and pushed away from the dock with an oar.

"So far so good," he whispered nervously to the terrified prisoner. "Frank will get there about an hour after you and I do. Ha ha! You're helping me into a high-paying Transport job, pal, so I guess the least I can do is kill you quick."

Tom had decided that the way to handle this evening's unthinkable work would be to evict his real personality and become, just for tonight, the kind of cold-eyed killer he had always admired in books; and he had found, to his somewhat uneasy surprise, that it wasn't too difficult to numb his mind and act automatically, without thinking. I'll just be a machine until this is over with, he kept telling himself.

The boat skimmed smoothly down the torch-lit Leethee tide, and none of the scavengers and beggars they passed gave the skiff a second look. Soon they passed through the last stone arch and found themselves in the harbor. The sun was only a hairsbreadth clear of the ocean's horizon, and the sky was a cathedral of terraced red-and-gold clouds against a background of pale blue.

"We're timing it well, my friend," Tom said, grinning jerkily as he turned the boat north. "Old Redbrick's ship ought to be just lowering anchor beyond the jetty. I'll kill you, knock out poor Frank, cut out his tongue and eyes and row him out to the ship." Tom thought he must have caught some subterranean ailment—he was nauseous and tense, and it required a constant effort to keep his eyes focused. "Redbrick will give me a hundred malories and take Frank away to the Tamarisk Isles. I'll take your headless body to Duprey, and tell him it's Frank, and he'll give me a job. Everybody does well except you, I guess. And, hell, a slave is probably happier dead

anyway, right?'' The slave moaned through his gag.
''That's right,'' agreed Tom.

He worked the boat north, around the anchored
merchant ships, until Frank's boat came into view.
He pulled alongside it, relieved to see no other boats
moored there.

''Up you go.'' Tom cackled, hoisting the slave
like an awkward piece of lumber onto the deck. He
followed, carrying the axe. ''Okay, you just lay there
for a minute. This is complicated, I admit, but if
we all do our parts it'll work out fine.''

The slave turned his face despairingly to the cabin
wall. Tom shrugged, put down the axe and went to
the door, which was locked; he kicked it open and
hurried into Frank's room, where he picked up a gray
shirt, a sword, a pair of shoes and a pair of white
corduroy pants. He bundled these together and went
out on deck again.

The bound slave still faced the wall, so Tom quietly set the clothes on the deck and picked up the
axe. He raised it over his head, aiming at the man's
neck. He stood that way for a while, squinting at the
horizon as if trying to remember something. Then his
attention returned to his surroundings, and with a
hearty grunt he swung the axe down with all the
force he could add to the thing's own weight, and he
crouched as he struck to keep the blow perpendicu-
lar. He stood up a moment later, rocked the blood-
splashed axe blade loose from the deck-wood it had
bitten into, and flung it overboard. The severed head
he tied in a canvas bag weighted with two sextants,
which he also tossed over the side.

He cut the ropes loose from the body and stripped
it of its clothes, and then pulled Frank's pants and
shirt onto it. The shoes were difficult—he pushed
them and pounded on the slave's feet, but to no

avail. He finally tossed the shoes into the sea. The sword clipped easily onto the belt, and Tom stood up dizzily.

He picked up the slave's bloodstained clothes, wrapped a large fishing sinker in them, and threw that bundle, too, into the water. It's a messy ocean floor tonight, he thought crazily. I wonder how often the cleaning lady comes.

He stumbled to the bow and sat down in one of the canvas deck chairs to await Frank's arrival. The sun was in Tom's eyes; no matter how he blinked and shifted his gaze he frequently got an eyeful of glare. Black spots floated through his vision. For this reason he didn't notice the approaching rowboat until it was only about fifty yards away.

"Oh no," he muttered. He stood up and waved, and then dashed back behind the cabin, crouched beside the headless body and rolled it over the rail into the sea. "I'll fish you out again real soon," he giggled. Then he ran back to the bow and waved again, smiling broadly.

"That's him," said one of the three men in the boat. "Look at him waving at us, all dressed in white. He must have mistaken us for someone."

"Yeah," agreed another. "I wonder why he ran away when he first saw us, though? Do you think it's a trap?"

"I don't know," said the third. "Best not to get too close, anyway. Move in ten yards more and I'll pitch a bomb at him."

A minute later the third man stood up, lit the fuse of a shot-put-sized bomb and hurled it at the larger boat. Tom still stood on the bow, waving. A moment later an explosion tore a hole in the cabin and flung pieces of lumber spinning through the air. The roar of the detonation echoed off the shore, and a cloud of smoke and wood splinters hung over the blasted vessel.

"Let's circle and look for the body," growled the man in the stern. The little rowboat made an unhurried circle around the smoking boat, and near the stern they found a headless body floating. They pulled it aboard.

"That's him all right. Odd the way the bomb just took his head off and left the rest of him untouched, though."

"Who cares?" said another. "It's him. Look, there's one of his shoes floating there. I've seen bombs do that. Let's get his body back to Costa quickly, and get paid." The other two nodded, and the one at the oars began leaning into his work.

An hour later Frank wearily tied up his own rowboat next to Tom's at the stern and climbed aboard. "Tom?" he called. "Sorry I'm late. Business, you know. Tom?" It was just light enough to see, and he looked in shock at the wreckage of his boat.

"Tom!" he shouted. "Where are you?" He leaped inside the cabin—and stared at the chaos he found. The bulkhead between the cabin and his own stateroom was split; the air was thick with the smell of gunpowder; his bed and desk lay shattered in the broken doorway, and stretched across this wreckage was a body. Frank crossed to it warily, and stared at the face.

He was just able to recognize it as Tom Strand's.

Frank backed out of the cabin and sat down heavily on the deck. My father, he thought. Orcrist. Blanchard. And now Tom. I'm poison to my friends, beyond doubt.

After a while he stood up and stared out to sea,

where a ship beyond the jetty was unfurling its sails
and tacking south.

It must be the Transports who did this, Frank
thought. They must have found out I was coming
here frequently, and thought Tom was me. He went
below and carried four bottles of Tamarisk brandy
into the cabin, then broke them on the floor. After he
dropped a lit match into the aromatic puddle and
heard it *whoosh* alight, he strode out onto the deck,
climbed into his rowboat and cast off.

HODGES lit a cigarette nervously. He liked times of
quiet prosperity, leisure to spend untroubled days
with his family and cats. It upset him to scent doom
in the air, and tonight it almost masked the tobacco
reek in his nostrils. He watched gloomily as Frank
poured himself a fifth glass of scotch.

"Gentlemen," Frank said, "remember that you
are . . . only my . . . *advisors*. I will listen, have
listened, to your timid cautions and warnings, and I
don't believe there's *any* course of action you'd favor. I've told you my idea, and you haven't yet given
me a good objection."

Hodges leaned forward. "Your plan, sire, is to try
out for the job of painting Costa's portrait and to kill
him once you get close to him. Right?"

"That's right, Hodges. You've got it. And then
I'll give a signal down the pipes somehow, which
will alert our sewer army. They'll be massed and
waiting in the tunnels somewhere, see. We've scav-
enged enough explosives to blow the floors out of
half the basements in the palace, and though the
Transports are prepared for possible attacks from
north, south, east, west and above, they aren't set up
to deal with one from *below*."

"I don't think *we* are, either," said a burly old

thief-lord known as Hussar. "You use the word *army*, Rovzar, but it's just an accumulation of bums and farmless farmers."

"We've been training them," Frank insisted, "and each one of them has a strong stake—namely his home and livelihood—in our being successful. And they'll be coming right up out of the cellars! Hell, we'll probably have the palace under our control before the guards on the walls even notice that anything has happened behind their backs."

"Well, Mr. Hussar has pointed out that you'd be killed yourself, almost immediately," said Hodges.

"I might not," Frank said, taking a liberal sip of his drink. "That doesn't matter, anyway. The main thing is to get rid of Costa."

"Ah. But who would they replace him with?"

"I don't know. A relative, if he has any—though God knows I can't find any. Who cares? It would be a change, anyway."

"Maybe not," Hodges answered. "Costa is only a figurehead for the Transport government. Kill him and they'll get another mascot. If you could kill the whole Transport there'd be a change—but killing poor idiot Costa would do nothing but give you personal vengeance, which a king can't really afford."

"Well, dammit, Hodges, I've got to do *something*. Every day we lie quiet, the Transport gets stronger. What's being done to stop them? I—"

"Sire," Hodges said, "Hemingway said never confuse motion with action. I think—"

"*I* think," said Hussar, leaning forward, "that perhaps we ought to discuss Mr. Rovzar's claim to be our king."

Hodges let the cigarette smoke hiss out between his teeth. Everyone had stopped talking, so the sound of Frank's sword sliding out of its sheath was clearly audible.

"How do you mean, Hussar?" asked Frank with a smile.

"Put your sword away," Hussar snapped angrily. "Tolley wasn't king when you killed him. Isn't that right, Hodges? Therefore, you can't claim the *ius gladii* precedent. Therefore you're not our king." Hussar sat back. "I wouldn't have brought this up," he added, "if you hadn't exhibited signs of alcoholism and insanity."

"Hodges," Frank said. "A point of protocol: what is the procedure when someone calls the king's qualifications into question?"

Hodges answered wearily, as if reciting a memorized piece. "The person is free to prove his allegations by engaging the king in personal combat. Sorry, Hussar."

Frank stood up, suddenly looking much soberer. His sword was in his hand. "Now, then, Hussar, what about these allegations?"

Hussar pressed his lips together angrily. "I withdraw them, sire," he said.

There was a long pause. "All right," Frank said finally. He sheathed his sword and sat down, looking vaguely puzzled and defeated. "I . . . I guess you're right, Hodges." He had another sip of scotch. "What we've got to do, I guess, is keep building our army and keep looking for a ducal heir." He drained his glass. "Keep sending the claimants to me, Hodges. Maybe if we don't find a real one we can come up with a convincing fake."

"A fake?" said Hodges. "Sire, even with a *real* one we'd have our work cut out for us." He shook his head. "Gentlemen, I pronounce this meeting adjourned." Everyone except Frank stood up and began shouldering on coats and bidding each other goodnight. They all filed out, leaving Frank alone in the room. Two of the lamps had gone out, the candles were low in their sockets, and the clink of the bottle-lip on the glass-edge, and the gurgle of the scotch sluicing into the glass, were the only sounds.

HEAVY music resounded in Kelly Harmon's huge living room, and most of the guests were dancing wildly. Harmon lived in the finest district of Munson Understreet, and his parties, which had become legendary in the belt-tightening days of Costa's reign, were said to be the gathering place of all the truly worthwhile people in Munson, above or below the surface. The music, provided by a trio of crazed trumpet players, was so loud that the knocking at the door could only be heard by the people actually leaning against it. They pulled the door open and a tall, dark-bearded man edged his way inside, waving an invitation, and was soon absorbed into the crowd.

The music and dancing slowly mounted in intensity to a feverish and frenzied climax, after which the dancers began reeling to their chairs and gulping drinks. Kathrin Figaro whirled like a spun top to the last choppy bars of one song, and collided with a table, knocking over a lamp.

"Whoops!" she giggled. "Time for a rest, I think." She weaved away from the dance floor to the only empty chair, at a back table at which the bearded man was sitting. "Can I join you?" she asked breathlessly. He looked up at her and, after the briefest hesitation, nodded.

"Thank you." She slid into the chair and looked at her table-mate. Long black hair was cut in uneven bangs across his forehead, and his eyes hid in a network of wrinkles under his brows. The black beard didn't quite hide a long scar that arched across his cheek. "Do I know you?" she asked politely, privately wondering how this derelict had got in.

"Yes," he said.

Kathrin looked at him uneasily. "Who are you?"

"John Pine."

Kathrin looked blank, and then startled. "*Frank ...?*" she whispered.

He nodded.

"But I heard you were dead—they hung . . . *somebody's* headless body, dressed in your clothes, from the palace wall a week ago." He shrugged impatiently. "When did you grow the beard, Frank? I don't like it."

"My name, *please*, is John Pine. The beard's fake."

"Oh." She lifted two glasses of champagne from the tray of a passing steward and set one of them before Frank. "Isn't it terribly risky for you to be here? Did you come to see me?"

"No," he said. "I didn't know you'd be here. I came because I was bored." He sipped the champagne. "Harmon has been sending me invitations to these affairs for months, and I decided to take him up on one."

"Will I see you at more of these, then?" she asked brightly.

"No. I'm not much of a party man, as you doubtless recall. And it *is* too risky a thing to make a habit of."

She tasted her drink thoughtfully. "Are you still king of the . . . you-know-whos?" He nodded. "I heard about how you got it. It sounded very brave." He looked at her skeptically. "I don't see Matthews anymore, John. He treated me horribly, just . . .

horribly. Do you think," she went on, lowering her eyes, "there's any chance of us trying it again?"

Yes, he thought. "No," he said.

"But I've—"

"Don't embarrass both of us, Kathrin." He stood up. "There's nothing to say. I shouldn't have come to this. I'm sorry." He stepped around the table, pushed his way through the crowd to the door and disappeared into the eternal understreet night.

THE yawning page boy plodded around the room, refilling the oil-reservoirs of the lamps from a can he carried. The job done, he returned to his chair, began nodding sleepily and was soon snoring.

George Tyler refilled Frank's wine glass and then his own; his aim had deteriorated during the evening, and he poured a good deal of it onto the tabletop.

"Frank," George said carefully, "don't try to pretend with *me* that this is an . . . altruistic action you're contemplating. You *know* that it isn't Costa that's strangling this planet. He's just a . . . pitiful puppet . . . within whom moves the cold, steely hand of the Transport." Pleased with his metaphor, Tyler chuckled and gulped his wine. "*And* it isn't even personal revenge, lad, that's goading you to kill the poor geek. Not entirely, anyway. Want to know what it is?"

"What is it, George?" Frank asked obligingly.

"It's suicide, Frankie," said Tyler sadly. "You want to die. No, don't get rude with me; I'm a poet, I'm allowed to talk this way. If you go grinning up to the palace gate with a knife in your paint box, it may look like a gallant bid for revenge, but *I'll* know. It will be a suicide attempt, disguised as desperate vengeance to fool everyone, yourself as well, maybe."

"George, you are so full of crap—"

"Yeah, you say that. But you're my last friend since Sam got it, and now you're *eager* to get killed. And all because that half-wit girl ditched you for Matthews."

"That isn't it, George. Not much of it, anyway."

"Aha! You admit it's suicide, then?"

"I'm not admitting anything, dammit. I'm humoring a raving drunk."

"Well, *there's* a judgment. But all right, I won't bother you anymore."

For a full five minutes they drank in silence.

"Someday I'll be restored to my former exalted state," Tyler muttered, half to himself, "and then I'll set all this right. I'll have Costa sweeping the gutters, and then you won't have to kill him."

"George," said Frank levelly, "I have been trying very hard, for weeks, to find a real claimant to the ducal throne. Throughout that time I have admired your tact in not burdening me with your own . . . delusions in that line. If there is (and there *is*) one thing I don't want to hear, it's another crackpot telling me he's the true prince."

"I'm sorry, Frank," Tyler said. "You're right, you don't need that." He emptied his glass. "I don't really believe all my stories, either, so you needn't think I'm a crackpot. It's just my poetic nature letting off steam."

"I didn't mean you're a crackpot, George. I spoke . . . heatedly, without thinking." Frank opened the table drawer and felt around in it, but his pipe was missing. "Where *did* you come up with all those stories about being Topo's son, anyway?" he asked.

"I made them up, mostly," Tyler said. "And my mother used to tell me I was. I was an illegitimate child, you see. I'll bet all unwed mothers tell their sons they're the secret offspring of royalty."

"Yeah, probably so. Not a good idea, in the long run, if you ask me." Frank poured out the last dribble of the bottle. "Page. Hey, page! Another bottle of this. A cold one."

The page nodded and scampered away.

"It was a bedtime story, you see," Tyler explained.

Frank hiccupped. "Did your mother even work in the palace? At least?"

"Naw, the story hasn't even got that much to support it. She told me she was a dancer at a tavern he used to go to. She claimed that for a season he was crazy about her, wanted to marry her. This would have been before Topo's brother, Ovidi, died, you see, back in the days when nobody thought Topo would ever make Duke. And Topo *was* supposed to be a wild lad in those days, you know, Frank—drunk all the time, always getting into fights—my mother told me he even got a tattoo of her, had it done on his chest by some young painter they both knew. The guy had never done a tattoo before, but he'd got hold of a tattooing needle somewhere, and they were all drunk, and so they gave it a try." Tyler smiled. "My mother said the tattoo didn't turn out too badly, considering."

Frank gulped some wine. "Oh?" he said. "That's good, that's a relief. Looked like her, did it? Caught a resemblance?"

Tyler laughed. "Well, no, probably not. He . . . portrayed her . . . in her dancing costume, which was . . . well, it was a bird suit."

Frank nodded. "A bird suit."

"Yeah, an immodest one. My mother didn't even describe it to me until I was fifteen. Her costume was an over-the-head bird mask, see, and big wings that she'd slip her arms down inside of—and nothing else. Well, shoes, maybe."

Frank laughed, but Tyler's words had reminded him of something. *Sure you don't want me to make it either all-bird or all-girl? I still could, you know.* His father had said that—to Duke Topo—who had never permitted himself to be seen even partially undressed.

"She even told me he'd made up a birth certificate for me, acknowledging me as a son of his. She said he'd shown it to her once, but wouldn't let her keep it, in case he changed his mind or something."

The page returned with the wine, and Frank absent-mindedly took a swig right from the bottle. "Uh," he said, noticing that his hand was shaking, "uh, this tattoo—"

"And you know where she said he'd *hid* this birth certificate?" Tyler went on. "You'll love this. In a copy of *Winnie the Pooh*. Frank! That's good wine!"

Frank had dropped the bottle, and pieces of wet glass spun on the floor. The page leaped up to fetch a mop and broom. "Never mind that," Frank told him. "Get Hodges for me. Tell him to summon a full council, at once. Yes, I know it's three o'clock in the morning. A full council, you hear? Immediately! Run!"

The page darted out of the room.

"Frank," said Tyler uncertainly, "are you all right?"

"For the first time in months, George."

An hour later twelve irritable lords sat around the table, their eyes squinting, their hair oddly tufted, and half of them in incorrectly-buttoned shirts.

"What is this, Hodges?" rasped Hussar. "More delirium tremens?"

"You're treading on thin ice, Hussar," said Hodges softly. "His majesty will be here in a moment to explain the reason for this meeting."

"We probably haven't been hijacking enough brandy to suit him," giggled Emsley.

"I'll discuss that with you afterward, if you like, Emsley," said Frank, who had silently entered the room. "Come on in, George."

Frank and Tyler took the two empty chairs at Hodges's left. "All right, gentlemen," Frank said. "I've found an heir—a genuine one, as a matter of fact. He's an illegitimate son of Topo, and I know where to find a birth certificate, signed by Topo, acknowledging him as a son."

The lords stared at him skeptically. Even Hodges looked doubtful, knowing that Frank had not interviewed any claimants since the last meeting. "And who is this lost prince?" asked Hussar, with a look of long-suffering patience.

"It's George Tyler," Frank said, knowing full well the response that declaration would have. It did. After a moment of stunned silence all the lords burst into howls of laughter.

"*Tyler?*" gasped Emsley. "Get some black coffee into you, Rovzar."

"Black coffee?" queried Frank with a quick smile. "Why black coffee, my lord?"

"Because you're drunk," Emsley replied carelessly.

"That will do, I think," Frank said, "especially in front of thirteen witnesses. You will do me the honor, Lord Emsley, of meeting me in East Watson Hall tomorrow morning at ten?"

Emsley paled. He glanced at Hussar, who was staring at the tabletop, and then at Frank. "But I—" he began. Frank raised his eyebrows. "All right," Emsley said weakly. "Ten o'clock."

"Now back to more important things," said Frank. "George, tell them about your bedtime story."

Tyler awkwardly outlined the story his mother used

to tell him, and told them where she'd claimed the
birth certificate was hidden.

"And Topo *did* have such a tattoo, gentlemen,"
said Frank, with a little more conviction than he actually felt, "and I know where that copy of *Winnie the
Pooh* is. I was with Topo when he was killed, and
just before the Transports kicked down the door, I
saw where he hid it."

"Where?" asked Hussar.

"In the throne room. For the time being I'll keep
to myself the exact hiding place. Now pay attention,
here is what we'll do: I'll assume a disguise and
apply for the job of painting Costa's portrait; I'm
confident that I'll get it. Once in the throne room I
will quietly remove the *Winnie the Pooh* from its
concealment, make an excuse to visit a bathroom,
and blow a loud whistle down the bathtub drain."

"And what will that do?" asked Hussar with exaggerated politeness.

"It will summon our army, which will be waiting
in the sewers under the Ducal Palace. They will
dynamite, from beneath, all the bathrooms, janitor
closets and laundry rooms in the cellars of the palace,
and attack through the resultant holes. I don't think
there's any doubt that we can take the palace. And
with an acknowledged prince to set on the throne, we
can hold it."

There was a thoughtful silence. "I think it's good,"
said Hodges finally. "I think it'll work."

"If you've got it right about this birth certificate,"
said Hussar cautiously, "I agree."

The others all nodded their somewhat qualified
approval, except for Emsley, who looked nauseous.

"With George on the throne we'll be able to evict
the Transport from Octavio," Frank said. "They
won't go cheerfully, but they haven't become strong

enough to openly oppose the government. In a year they *would* be strong enough. I suggest, therefore, that we mount our attack on the day after tomorrow, first to strike before they get any stronger, and second to prevent them from hearing about it in advance.''

"This seems hasty, your majesty . . ." began Hodges.

"It's quick, Hodges, but it isn't hasty. Now send me maps of the palace sewers, and their connections with the understreet sewers. You'll all be hearing from me tomorrow (later today, I should say), so be where I can reach you. And Hodges," added Frank as they all stood up, "since it looks like I'm going to get no sleep tonight, bring me a pot of black coffee, will you?"

For the next three hours, Frank studied multi-level sewer diagrams and drawings of the palace, making copious notes and drinking quantities of coffee. Finally he threw down his pen and rubbed his bloodshot eyes.

"I think I see how we'll do it," he said to Hodges, who was lighting his twelfth cigarette since the meeting. "The palace sewers all run into a long watercourse that joins the Leethee near the Bailey District. That's the most direct route, and it shouldn't be hard for you to get the army organized there. Then you run them up the line and into the pipes that connect with the palace. The pipes are all five feet high and probably well built, since they date from the time of Duke Giroud. Then you'll just wait for the whistle."

"Sounds good to me, sire," said Hodges a little sleepily.

Frank sat back and drained his most recent cup of coffee. "Hodges?"

"Yes, sire?"

''Was the Subterranean Companions' meeting hall ever a church?''

Hodges blinked. ''Uh, yes. A couple of hundred years ago some philanthropist built two churches understreet. He later disappeared—some say he ascended bodily into heaven, some say he fell into the Leethee.'' Hodges took a long puff on the cigarette and exhaled slowly. ''So one of his churches became our meeting hall, and one, to the northwest, was converted into a cheap hotel. It was destroyed, incidentally, when that bomb took out four levels last year. The place had two carved-iron gates out front, said to have been cast by some sculptor of note. They both fell into the Leethee flood when the explosion kicked the place apart. Haven't been found yet.''

''Ah.'' Frank reached for the coffee pot. ''Well, I've got to figure out the arrangement of our troops, Hodges, but you can go home. Get some sleep; we'll all be busy as hell later today.''

''Right. Thank you, sire.''

Chapter 3

Thirty miles northwest of Munson—separated from the city by slums, suburbs, small cities and, eventually, the most wealthy neighborhoods on the planet—stood the Ducal Palace, a grim fortress of centuries-old stone under the bright banners that waved from its walls.

The sun had made dust of the spring mud, and the merchants who thronged the gate and courtyard wore veils across their noses and mouths. Street musicians fiddled and clanged at every corner, storytellers babbled to rings of children, and palace guards fingered their sweat-damp sword grips and squinted irritably at the crowds. The place was a carnival of smells: garlic, curried meat, dust, sweat, hot metal and exotic tobacco.

Under the barbican, across the bridge and through the gate plodded a tall man on a gray horse. The man wore a ragged brown leather jacket and a white cape, and had wrapped a length of white cloth around his

head and across his lower face, so that only his cold
blue eyes, a glimpse of a scar and a lock or two of
black hair showed. He was unarmed, and carried
only a wooden box slung behind him on the saddle.

Whichever way it falls today, Frank thought, this
is the end of a circular road I've travelled for a year.
It's been a busy year, too—I've been an art forger, a
thief, a kitchen boy, a fencing teacher and a king of
thieves. I've fallen in love, and climbed out of it.
And I've seen more deaths—of friends, enemies and
strangers—than I want to think about.

He nudged his tired horse across the crowded courtyard to the steps of the keep.

"What's your business, stranger?" asked the guard,
a red-faced man in the ubiquitous Transport uniform.

Frank unwrapped the white cloth from his head
and shook back his hair. An artificial moustache
clung to his upper lip. "I've come to paint the Duke's
portrait," he said. "I understand he wants it done."

"Yeah, that's true, he does. Leave your horse here
and go down the hall inside. Third door on your left.
Are you armed?"

"No. I'm a painter."

"Well, open up your box and let me see."

Frank unstrapped his battered wooden box and
handed it to the guard, who set it down on the dusty
pavement and flipped up its lid. He rummaged about
for a few seconds in the brushes, crumpled tubes and
bottles, and then closed it and gave it back.

"Okay," he said. "Go on in. Third on your left."

Frank dismounted and let a footman lead his horse
away, then picked up his box and walked up the
steps into the keep. The third door on the left opened
easily when Frank turned the knob, revealing a counter
behind which a dozen people sat at paper-littered
desks. An old man shambled up to the counter.

"You're applying for the custodial position?" he asked.

"No," Frank said. "I've come to paint Duke Costa's portrait."

"Oh. Okay. Wait on that bench for a moment."

Five minutes later a grinning, slick-haired clerk approached. "You've brought your portfolio, yes?"

"No," Frank said, "but I'll draw you in two minutes."

The man raised an eyebrow. "Go ahead."

Frank took a chewed pencil from a pocket in his leather jacket. He laid his box across his knees and quickly sketched the man, using the side of the box for a surface. The drawing was quick and graceful, shaded with the fine cross-hatching of which his father had been master.

"Hm," said the official, peering at it. "Not bad. But can you paint? It's a painting he wants, you know."

"Paint. Sure." Frank took three tubes of paint, all shades of brown, out of his box and squeezed blobs from them onto the bench. He dipped a brush in one and went to work on the wall. In five minutes there glistened on the ancient plaster a portrait, done in the style of Goya, of the slick-haired clerk.

"Well," said the clerk, "you're good enough for me to pass you on to the Duke for a final decision, but I'm afraid I'll have to fine you five malories for defacing government property."

"Take it out of my salary," Frank said. "When can I start on the portrait?"

"Anytime, I guess. I'll have a guard escort you to the throne room, and you can discuss it with the Duke himself. Uh, what's your name?"

"Richard Helder," Frank told him. The clerk scribbled it on a piece of paper, then handed it to a guard.

"Just follow him, Mr. Helder," the clerk said. Frank nodded his thanks and followed the guard upstairs.

The throne room, as Frank noticed when he was finally admitted, had changed considerably during his absence. The bookcases and desk were gone, replaced by overly-colorful tapestries, the throne had been painted, and the year-old, unfinished Claude Rovzar portrait of Duke Topo was nowhere to be seen.

Duke Costa, a little redder of face and ampler of belly, was sitting on the throne and staring at a sheaf of star-maps. "Who's that?" he asked the guard, pointing at Frank.

"An artist," said the guard. "Richard Helder. Briggs passed him."

"I'll be with you in a moment," Costa smiled, returning to his star-maps. Frank nodded and sat down in a chair by the entrance. He glanced at the doors and saw, dimly under the new paint, the unevenness of the putty filling in the old bullet holes.

The rise and fall of Duke Costa, Frank thought. Or maybe the rise and fall of Frank Rovzar. This is the room our fathers died in.

Under this building, he thought, staring at the floor, crouches, silently, my army. It would be an interesting development if the army *wasn't* down there—if they've simply stayed home, as Emsley told them to do yesterday, just before I killed him.

Idly, as he waited, Frank did a couple of sketches of Costa in profile on the reverse side of the paint box.

Finally Costa flung the maps aside. "Mr. Helder?" he said. "I understand Briggs likes your work. He's not too easily pleased. What were you drawing there, just a second ago?"

Frank walked forward and showed the Duke the profiles.

"Not bad," Costa said with a critical squint. "I like the style. Did you ever study the works of Rovzar?"

"What artist hasn't?" replied Frank.

"Just so," nodded Costa. "When can you begin?"

"That depends," said Frank in an artificially casual voice. "You see, the only canvases I have are small—fit for paintings of children, or kittens, but hardly Dukes. I can order a canvas, of course; but with the interplanetary shipping system in the state it's in, God knows when it would come." He hoped Costa was unaware that canvases were made on Octavio. "Uh . . . you wouldn't happen to *have* an old canvas, a painting, lying around, that I could paint over? Something roughly three feet by five feet?"

"By God, I have!" laughed Costa. "Hey, guard!" he yelled. "Bring that picture in here! The big unfinished one!" He grinned at Frank. "You, sir," he said, "are to have the privilege of painting over a genuine unfinished Rovzar."

Frank raised his eyebrows, but didn't say anything.

The painting was brought in, still on the original easel. It was dimmed with dust, and something greasy had dripped down the left side of it, but Frank easily recognized his father's work, and the sight of it brought back memories of the old man with more force than anything else had in a year.

The guards bowed and withdrew. Frank took a rag out of his paint box and gently wiped off the canvas. There, looking nobler than Frank had ever seen him look in life, sat Duke Topo. Frank reached out and ran his fingers over the fine brush strokes.

He turned to Costa to speak, but saw the Duke,

suddenly pale, rising from the throne and pointing a
trembling finger at him. "I . . . I was told you were
dead," he whispered.

"You've got me confused with someone," said
Frank levelly.

"No, no. Your drawing style—I should have
guessed immediately." The Duke slid his jewel-hilted
rapier out of its velvet scabbard and then ran at Frank
with the weapon held over his head like an axe.
Frank snatched up the paint box and caught the descending blade with it; the sword stuck, and Frank
roughly levered it out of Costa's grasp. He kicked the
Duke in the stomach and Costa dropped to the floor.
Frank wrenched the paint-smeared blade loose, raised
it—Costa cowered under an upflung arm—and brought
it down across the face of the painting, slashing the
canvas open from top to bottom.

"Guards!" bellowed Costa, scuttling away from
him like a frightened beetle. "I'm being killed!"

Frank reached in behind the split painting and
seized the book, then ran to the door just as it was
flung open by the first of four sword-waving Transport guards.

Frank drove the spattered rapier at one of them,
who parried it hard, flinging drops of color at the
wall. The *Winnie the Pooh* was in Frank's right
hand, so he hit the man in the face with it. A sword
tore a gash in Frank's right shoulder, and he twisted
around and cut the throat of the guard who held it.
Then he was through them, and running to find a
bathroom. He impatiently peeled off the itchy false
moustache and flung it to the ground.

"Get him! Get him!" screamed Costa. "He's
insane!"

Frank ducked into one room and surprised a half-
dozen women who were tacking typed pages onto a

bulletin board; he fled them and their panicky, guard-drawing screams and dashed down another hallway. Blood from his shoulder spotted his cape and ran down his arm onto the leather binding of the book he held.

Ahead of him a guard appeared from around a corner. The man raised his arm and a bang sounded as a strip of plaster beside Frank's head turned to powder. Frank convulsively kicked open the nearest door, ran through the room beyond it and, whirling his cape over his head, leaped through the closed window.

He fell, together with a rain of shattered glass, through fifteen feet of air onto pavement, rolling as he landed to minimize the impact. He tore his cape off, picked up his book and sword and looked around. He was in an enclosed garden; tables stood among the greenery, and astonished people were flinging down forks and getting to their feet; two guards, swords out, strode toward him.

Frank desperately picked up a chair from beside a nearby table and tossed it through the largest ground-floor window, which burst inward with a hideous racket. Frank leaped through it, hearing the shouts of guards from all sides. I'll never get to a bathroom now, he thought dizzily. They've got me surrounded.

He was in a bar-lounge occupied only by a sparse midmorning crowd. He vaulted over the bar, scattering glasses and ashtrays, and sent the bartender sprawling with a blow of his sword-pommel. Then, lying under the bar sink, he fumbled in his pocket and put a powerful whistle to his lips, and blew it with all the strength he could wring out of his lungs directly into the floor-drain.

"Where is he?" someone called excitedly.

"He's hiding behind the bar!" howled the bartender, who had run off while Frank was blowing the whistle.

"All right, Pete, bring your boys in from the left, and we'll go in from the right. We may be able to get him alive."

Frank blew his whistle twice more, cupping his hands around the drain to aim the noise downward.

"The Duke's right," someone called. "He *is* crazy. He's trying to play music back there."

Frank took hold of his sword, stuffed the book in his shirt and stood up. A dozen of them. Here's where I die, possibly. "What'll it be, gents?" he asked with a smile.

They charged—and simultaneously the wall behind them exploded into the room like a gravel pile kicked by a giant. Frank was hurled backward into a display case of bottles, and two of the Transports landed on top of him. After the debris had stopped falling he flung their limp bodies aside and struggled to his feet, coughing in the dust-foggy air. He heard the roars of two more explosions; and a third; and a fourth.

The silhouettes of men moved behind the rubble of the wall. "Hey!" Frank called, waving his sword. "This way, Companions! I'm Rovzar!"

The men cheered and ran to him, led by Hussar. "Should have known I'd find you in the bar," the lord grinned.

"We've got to get upstairs," Frank said. "Costa's up there. Come on." Every second, more men were climbing out of the hole in the foundation where the ladies' room had been, but Frank impatiently hustled the first ten out of the bar and up the first flight of stairs they came to.

They met three guards on the stairs; two died and the third fled upstairs, hotly pursued. Yells, cheers and explosions echoed up and down the corridors. Frank's band of Companions took off after the fleeing Transport, but Frank concentrated on his search for the Duke. After a few minutes of running and dodging he saw, at the end of a corridor, the two doors of the throne room. He ran toward them and launched a flying kick that ripped the bolt out of the wood on the other side. The doors slammed inward, knocking over a Transport guard and startling six others. Behind them all stood Costa, radiating both fear and rage.

"There he is, idiots!" he yelled. "Get him, quickly!"

Frank ran at the six guards and, with only a token preparatory feint, drove his point through one man's throat. He parried a downward-sweeping blade with his right arm, and winced as the edge bit through the leather jacket into his skin; then he riposted with a quick jab between the ribs and the man rolled to the floor, more terrified than hurt. Two Transports now engaged Frank's blade while a third man ran in and swung a whistling slash into Frank's belly. The impact knocked Frank off his feet and the guards cheered as their adversary fell.

"Finish him, finish him!" screeched Costa, waving a rapier he'd picked up.

The foremost guard raised his sword as if he were planting a flag, and drove it savagely downward into—the floor, for Frank had rolled aside. Pausing only to hamstring another guard, he scrambled catlike to his feet. His shirt was cut across just above the belt, and the *Winnie the Pooh* had been chopped nearly in half.

Costa, beginning to worry about the outcome of the skirmish, tore down one of his gaudy tapestries and opened a door it had hidden. Frank saw him step

through it, and swung a great arc with his blade to
make the Transports jump back a step—like most
novice swordsmen, they were more fearful of the
dramatic edge than the deadlier but less spectacular
point—and then leaped for the secret door, catching
it a moment before it would have clicked shut. He
hopped through before the four remaining guards got
to it, and shot the bolt just as they began wrenching
and pounding on the door from the other side.

He turned; a narrow stairway rose before him, and
he could hear Costa's quick steps ahead and above.
Frank gripped his sword firmly and loped up the
stairs two at a time. He was very tired—near exhaustion, really—and he was losing blood from his right
shoulder and forearm; but he wanted to settle the
issue with Costa before he rested. He kept thinking
about the night at the Doublon Festival when he had
seen Costa's face over the barrel of a pistol, and had
failed to pull the trigger.

At the top of the stairs stood an open arch that
framed a patch of the blue sky. Leaping through it
Frank found himself on the slightly tilted red-tile roof
of the palace. The stairway arch he'd come out of
stood midway between two chimneys that marked the
north and south edges of the roof. Resting against the
northern chimney was Costa, staring hopelessly at
the spot where, before all the explosions started, a
fire escape had stood.

Frank slowly walked toward him, and Costa stood
clear of the chimney and raised his sword in a salute.
After a moment of hesitation, Frank returned the
salute. Plumes of black smoke curled up into the sky
from below, and the roof shook under their feet from
time to time as more bombs went off within the
building.

Neither man said anything; they paused, and then

Costa launched a tentative thrust at Frank's face. Frank parried it easily but didn't riposte—he was in no hurry and he wanted to get the feel of the surface they were fighting on. The tiles, he discovered as he cautiously advanced and retreated across them, were too smooth to get traction on, and frequently broke and slid clattering over the edge.

Frank feinted an attack to Costa's outside line and then drove a lunge at the Duke's stomach; Costa parried it wildly but successfully and backed away a few steps. A cool wind swept across the roof, drying the sweat on Frank's face. His next attack started as an eye-jab but ducked at the last moment and cut open the back of the Duke's weapon hand. That ought to loosen his grip, Frank thought, as another explosion rocked the building.

Costa seemed upset by the blood running up his arm, so Frank redoubled the attack with a screeching, whirling bind on the Duke's blade that planted Frank's sword-point in Costa's cheek. The Duke flinched and retreated another step, so that he was once again next to the north chimney.

"Checkmate, Costa," Frank said, springing forward in a high lunge that threatened Costa's face; Costa whipped his sword up to block it—and Frank dropped low, driving his sword upward through Costa's velvet tunic, ample belly and pounding heart.

The transfixed Duke took one more backward step, overbalanced and fell away into the empty air, the sword still protruding from his stomach.

Frank stood up and brushed the sweat-matted hair out of his face with trembling fingers. Time to go below, he thought; too bad Costa took both swords down with him.

He turned to the stairway arch—and a final, much more powerful explosion tore through all three stories beneath him and blew the north wall out in a rain of dissolving bricks. The whole north half of the roof crumbled inward, and Frank, riding a wave of buckling, shattering tiles, disappeared into the churning cloud of dust and cascading masonry as timbers, furniture, sections of walls and a million free-falling rocks thundered down onto the unpaved yard of the list.

Epilogue: The Painter

Kiowa Dog and his friends were bored. The scaffolding around the north end of the palace was fenced off, so they couldn't play there. It was too hot and dusty to play tag or knife-the-bastard, so they sat in the shade of a melon cart and flicked pebbles at the legs of passing horses.

"Let's *do* something," said Cher-cher.

"Like what?" asked Kiowa Dog lazily.

"We could go explore the cellar."

"I'm sick of your damned cellar," Kiowa Dog explained.

"Well, we could climb—holy cow, Kiowa, look at this guy!" Cher-cher pointed at a bizarre figure leaving the keep and heading slowly for the open palace gates.

It was a man, riding in a small donkey cart because his left leg had been amputated at the hip. His age was impossible to judge—his thick hair was a youthful shade of black, and his body was that of an

213

active young man, but his lined face and scarred
cheek implied a greater age. He wore a bronze ear,
and it glittered and winked in the sunlight as the cart
bumped over the cobblestones.

"What circus are you from, Jack?" yelled Kiowa
Dog.

"Juggle for us! Dance!" giggled Cher-cher.

FRANK didn't hear the children's calls. He sat back
in his cart, enjoying the sunlight and the glow of the
wine he'd had with breakfast. He reached behind to
make sure his supplies—his new paint box, several
canvases, four bottles of good rosé from the ducal
cellar—were still strapped down in the shaded back
of the cart, and then lightly flicked the reins. The
donkey increased his pace slightly.

It hasn't been smooth and it hasn't been nice, he
thought, this circle I've walked for a year—but it's
closed now. He remembered his father's saying: "If
it was easy, Frankie, they'd have got somebody else
to do it." Well, Dad, it must be easy, because I think
they are getting somebody else to do it.

ON A second-floor balcony of the keep, a man in a
blue silk robe watched the donkey cart's progress
toward the gate.

"So long, Frank," he whispered.

"I beg your pardon, your grace?" spoke up the
page standing behind him.

"Never mind," Tyler snapped. "Uh . . . bring me
the Transport file on Thomas Strand, will you?"

The page bowed and sprinted away down a hall.

I guess you were right to leave, Tyler thought.
There's nothing left for you here, above or below
ground. Maybe there is a life for you in the hills, as
you said.

Tyler pounded his fist once, softly on the railing. You should have thought of it, Frank. Gunpowder and dynamite are more valuable than gold. Where else would a stupid, suspicious man like Costa store it but in the palace basement? And then your ignorant understreet thugs come up from below with their own explosives. . . . I've never seen a book as ruined as that *Winnie the Pooh* was when we dug it and you out of the wreckage: cut, ripped, smashed and blood-soaked, but still carrying intact its precious document.

The page returned, holding a manila folder. "Thank you," Tyler said, dismissing the boy with a wave. He opened the file and read Captain Duprey's notes and reports. After a few minutes of reading he nodded, as if the file had confirmed certain suspicions, and struck a match. The folder was slow to catch fire, but burned well once it did, and a few moments later Tyler dropped the blackened, flickering shreds and let the wind take them.

"I won't take any of your friends from you, Frank," he said. "Especially the dead ones."

THE crowd in front of the Ducal Palace bored Frank Rovzar, and he kept his eyes on the hills beyond. I could ride east, he thought. The Goriot Valley is being farmed again, and the country is lush with vineyards and hospitable inns and friendly peasant girls.

He smiled, deepening the lines in his cheeks. No, he thought, it's the western hills for me, the occasional towns among the yellow fields and the gray-brown tumbleweed slopes. It's a dry region but it's my father's country, and it's there, if anywhere, that I'll be able to practice the craft I was born and named for.

AFTERWORD

This is my first book. I wrote it ten years ago, in 1975, and its sale was excuse enough for me to quit college—high time, after six years!—and quit my pizza-cook-&-dishwasher job too. I had got my very first rejection slip ten years before that, when I was thirteen, so quitting school and work now seemed to have a fitting symmetry about it. (Later I did have to go back to the job, but at least I never went back to school.)

For this printing I've had to go through the book and touch it up—tighten it here, shore it up better there, trim some stuff I can now recognize as unnecessary—and it's been a surprisingly nostalgic experience to get back into the workings of the book after all these years, like digging up a homemade lawn sprinkler system you laid down a decade ago: you see which materials have lasted, you see places for improvements you should have thought of then, you find forgotten initials scrawled into the concrete when it was still wet, and what's this, a set of car keys with a key for that old motorcycle I used to ride to school on.

Let me tell you why I write. I can watch *E.T.*, or listen to Bob Marley and the Wailers, or eat sashimi with wasabi and soy sauce and that stuff that seems to be grated radish, and just be grateful that I frequently have the money to avail myself of them and happen to live in a world where such things exist; but when I finish reading a fine book—*The Shining*, say, or MacDonald's *A Deadly Shade of Gold*, or Amis's *Girl, 20*—I'm left with an uneasy feeling that simply having paid my three dollars wasn't enough. Like the primitive cargo cults who build straw replicas of the airplanes they see flying past overhead, I want to express my gratitude by *doing it too*. I suppose if I were a distiller I'd feel this way when I tasted Laphroaig or Wild Turkey or Plymouth gin.

So I can clearly see, when I reread this, what sorts of stories I was grateful for in 1975; science fiction, of course (I first read Heinlein's *Red Planet* when I was eleven), and adventure and swordfights (I think you could rub the flat of a sharp pencil point over any page of this book and read "Raphael Sabatini"), and a bit of low humor in the pull-the-chair-out-from-under-the-fat-boy vein (*The Three Musketeers*, Dumas's rendition or Richard Lester's, has always delighted me).

You know, it occurs to me that my tastes haven't improved a bit in ten years. In fact, just to show you how little I've learned, this summer I quit my job again.

This book always seems to have that effect on me.
Wish me luck!

—Tim Powers
July, 1985

GORDON R. DICKSON

☐	53068-3	Hoka! (with Poul Anderson)	$2.95
	53069-1		Canada $3.50
☐	53556-1	Sleepwalkers' World	$2.95
	53557-X		Canada $3.50
☐	53564-2	The Outposter	$2.95
	53565-0		Canada $3.50
☐	48525-5	Planet Run	$2.75
		with Keith Laumer	
☐	48556-5	The Pritcher Mass	$2.75
☐	48576-X	The Man From Earth	$2.95
☐	53562-6	The Last Master	$2.95
	53563-4		Canada $3.50
☐	53550-2	BEYOND THE DAR AL-HARB	$2.95
	53551-0		Canada $3.50
☐	53558-8	SPACE WINNERS	$2.95
	53559-6		Canada $3.50
☐	53552-9	STEEL BROTHER	$2.95
	53553-7		Canada $3.50